S.

THE LIFE AND TIMES
OF CHRISTMAS CALVERT...ASSASSIN

THE LIFE AND TIMES OF CHRISTMAS CALVERT ...ASSASSIN

John Wainwright

Chivers Press
Bath, Avon, England

•

G.K. Hall & Co.
Thorndike, Maine USA

This Large Print edition is published by Chivers Press, England, and by G.K. Hall & Co., USA.

Published in 1996 in the U.K. by arrangement with Little, Brown and Company.

Published in 1996 in the U.S. by arrangement with Little, Brown and Company.

U.K. Hardcover ISBN 0–7451–2890–4 (Chivers Large Print)
U.K. Softcover ISBN 0–7451–2897–1 (Camden Large Print)
U.S. Softcover ISBN 0–7838–1473–9 (Nightingale Collection Edition)

The text of this Large Print edition is unabridged.
Other aspects of the book may vary from the original edition.

Set in 16 pt. New Times Roman.

Printed in Great Britain on acid-free paper.

British Library Cataloguing in Publication Data available

Library of Congress Cataloging-in-Publication Data

Wainwright, John William, 1921–
   The life and times of Christmas Calvert—Assassin / John Wainwright.
     p. cm.
   ISBN 0–7838–1473–9 (lg. print : lsc)
   1. Large type books.   I. Title.
[PR6073.A354L54   1996]
823'.914—dc20
                                              95–31076

THE LIFE AND TIMES
OF CHRISTMAS CALVERT ... ASSASSIN

If you stand with your back to the 'Crazy Golf' course—facing out, across the prom and looking over the Irish Sea—you will see the South Pier directly ahead of you. To the right of the pier-head entrance you will see a form. It faces the prom railings, and has the prom traffic at its rear. It is a slatted, cast-iron-legged invitation to a temporary rest.

The man sat on this bench.

He was alone. It was mid-November. The strong breeze, from the West, had a raw bite to it; the icy drizzle came down in regular clouds of wetness. Farther along the prom, the council workers were using a yellow, platform-lift truck in order to dismantle the recently switched-off illuminations.

The man wore a battered deerstalker, a heavy, roll-necked sweater, a high-collared windcheater, corduroy trousers and thick-soled, US-Army, laced boots.

There was a stillness about the man. A tranquillity. The impression was that, had the weather changed to hurricane ferocity, the man would have remained motionless; deep in his own thoughts; impervious to the elements or, indeed, to any outside forces.

He didn't move. He didn't even blink his eyes. He exuded an air of massive strength. Of immense will-power. Of a complete lack of human frailty.

He was remembering.

His memories went back more than half a century. To this same bench—or to its predecessor—and to himself. Still alone. Still a creature of great self-sufficiency. Still neither sad—nor happy ... nor *anything*.

He leaned forward slightly; both hands resting, lightly, on the silver grip of the malacca-like cane.

His eyes—cornflower-blue eyes, within a web of age- and weather-lines—staring, unblinkingly at the horizon. Giving no hint that he had noticed the woman walking quietly along the prom, from the direction of the Sandcastle, and getting nearer with every step.

She reached the bench, and sat on his left.

For all of three minutes, neither spoke. Neither moved.

The woman was wearing a fur coat, with the collar turned up against the weather. She wore tight gloves and carried an expensive-looking handbag. The light flow of traffic passed behind them. An occasional pedestrian, head bent against the weather, hurried along the prom. The woman sat with her handbag on her knees. The man sat with his hands resting on the grip of the cane.

The woman opened her handbag and dipped her gloved hand inside.

The man moved with terrifying speed and

smoothness.

A twist on the cane's grip. A pull and then a flick to the left. The needle point of the foot-and-a-half-long steel, with its surgically sharpened edge, pricked the wrist of the glove, before the woman had time to pull her hand from the handbag.

A tiny pearl of crimson grew on the surface of the glove material.

The woman froze into immobility.

The man said, 'As I recall, you often carry a derringer in that bag of yours.'

The woman's lips moved into the ghost of a smile.

'Keep the hand empty,' said the man. 'Slowly. Gently. Unless, of course, you're anxious to have the arm skewered to your side.'

The woman withdrew her hand from the bag, and, all the time, the blade remained with its point beneath the surface of the skin.

When the hand was clear, the man reached across with his free hand and lifted a Colt No.4 derringer from the bag and in a single, fluid movement, sent it spinning over the prom railing and into the almost full tide.

'Now,' he said, 'we can relax.'

He re-sheathed the short sword-stick and the woman pressed a thumb over the tiny wound, without taking either hand out of its glove.

'Would you have used it?' he asked.

She hesitated then, in a solemn, very sincere voice, said, 'It's not impossible. Had it been

3

necessary.'

They spoke in cultured voices, but it was not the culture of a public school. Neither of them drawled. Nor was there even a hint of 'university' pronunciation. Rather it was the speech of the self-educated. Not far removed from the nigh-deliberate articulation of the elocution class.

She said, 'I doubted whether you'd come.'

'I said I would.'

'Your promises were never worth much, I'm afraid.'

'To you ... surely?'

She took a deep breath. Indeed, it might have been mistaken for a sigh.

She said, 'Where is she, Chris?'

'If I said I don't know?'

'I wouldn't believe you.'

The man moved his shoulders slightly, and instead of answering her implied criticism, said, 'Do you remember? Fifty years ago ... thereabouts? I was sitting here. On this form. And you came towards me from the open air swimming baths.'

'I remember.'

'So young. So innocent.'

'Then, I *might* have believed you.'

1940

The man sat on the bench.

He was a young man—barely out of his teens—and the RAF uniform fitted him badly. It was a uniform stiff with newness and with the 'heaviness' peculiar to livery fresh from government stores. The boots, too, were of heavy, chrome leather, polished to a glass-smooth sheen and worn awkwardly. As if the man was more used to more pliable footwear.

He was sweating a little, which wasn't surprising, as the June sun blazed its heat down upon a town which still catered for holidaymakers.

The man sat on the bench and faced seawards. He idly watched people on the stretch of sand exposed by the outgoing tide; the cluster of donkeys which, despite the war, continued to offer short rides to holidaying kids; the adverts on the pier pavilion inviting audiences to the evening performances of the Arcadian Follies—Harry Koris, Albert Modley, a complete change of programme every Thursday.

The man had never been to Blackpool before. He'd never been to the coast before. He still had that look of wonderment with which he'd first viewed the brash assemblage of theatres, cinemas, fun fairs, cheapjack stalls, hotels, boarding houses, sand and sea. He was still undecided about whether or not he liked what he saw.

The war had been in progress less than a year but, already, the promenade was one vast, elongated parade ground. More than half the boarding houses and not a few of the hotels had been requisitioned by the RAF and, daily, more recruits arrived to be inoculated, vaccinated, drilled, lectured to, shouted at and generally stripped of their civilian personalities and, instead, forced into the matrix of service ways and mannerisms.

The Pleasure Beach still functioned at full swing. The roar of the Big Dipper and the screams of the riders were merely a foreground sound to the background noise of fairground music, shouting and laughter. Despite the war—despite the inconvenience of the blackout regulations—it was still 'holiday season' and Blackpool continued to cater for those with money to spend on packaged happiness, and the recruits and the holidaymakers mixed and laughed together as if the world was still at peace and Adolf Hitler had yet to be born.

To the man's left—beyond the pier-head entrance, and crouched behind its barrier of artificial rocks and tarmac paths—the open air swimming pool gleamed its white marble and poked its high-diving boards at the cloudless sky.

The WAAF sergeant marched briskly along one of these paths. She came from the large car park at the south end of the swimming baths. She held herself well and moved as if filled with vigour and self-importance. She marched up the path and onto the prom, past the pier-head and past the opening in the railings which gave entry to the beach. She glanced at her wrist-watch, and seemed satisfied.

She stopped at the bench, and spoke to the young man sitting there.

'A. C. Calvert?'

'Eh?' The young man seemed surprised, and blinked up at the WAAF sergeant.

'Are you Aircrafthand Second Class Calvert?'

'Oh—er—yes. Yes. That's me.'

Calvert jumped to his feet and, for a split second, made as if he was going to salute the WAAF.

The WAAF said, 'Come with me, please. The wing commander wants to see you.'

The WAAF turned and returned the way she had come. Calvert followed her. Past the open air swimming pool and back to the car park. She held the door of a Humber open for him, then climbed behind the wheel. She looked too small—too frail—to handle a car of that size, but she handled the vehicle with a certain panache. She swung left onto the prom, then sped north, past the Central and North piers, past the Tower, past the Palace, and at last she swung right and into the car park of the Imperial Hotel.

As he climbed from the car she said, 'We'll go straight to his room. He's expecting us.'

He followed her into the luxury hotel, through the foyer and up the stairs leading to the upper floors. Part way along a carpeted corridor she tapped at a door. A voice came from inside and the WAAF opened the door to reveal an office, complete with a king-sized desk, steel filing cabinets, wall-graphs and -maps and a scattering of chairs. The room was obviously part of a suite of rooms and had, apparently, been taken over by the RAF. The man behind the desk was middle-aged, heavy jowled, running to fat and almost bald. He wore uniform with the broad band of wing commander at the cuffs. He also sported the 'Pip Squeak and Wilfred' ribbons of World War One.

The WAAF said, 'Calvert, sir.'

The wing commander said 'Ah, yes.' He waved a slightly imperious hand in dismissal and added, 'Thank you. Leave us, sergeant.' The WAAF left, closing the door, and the wing commander said, 'Right, Calvert. Take a seat. We need to exchange opinions.'

The bewildered Calvert muttered, 'Yes, sir,' then obeying the waved signals of the wing commander's hand, pulled a chair from its place by the wall, and positioned it at the desk, opposite the officer.

8

'Sit down,' said the wing commander, as if anxious to impress the fact that things were not strictly 'official'.

And, when Calvert was seated, the wing commander opened a slim manila file, consulted the contents, looked up, across the desk, and spoke.

'Calvert. Christmas Calvert? *Christmas?*'

'Yes, sir.'

'An unusual first name ... wouldn't you say?'

'It's—er—when I was found, sir. During the Christmas period.'

'Found?'

'I was abandoned, then adopted, sir.'

'Oh!'

'I don't know who my parents are.' He hesitated, then added, 'I was left in a clothes basket. In the waiting room, at Leeds Central Station.'

'Ah!' The wing commander cleared his throat, then asked, 'How long have you been in the Air Force, Calvert?'

'Three weeks, sir. Three weeks, tomorrow.'

'You volunteered, of course.'

'Oh, yes sir. I'm only nineteen, sir. I—er—I'd like to fly, sir. Eventually.'

'Really?' The wing commander's voice carried the hint of gentle mockery. Then, 'I see you were—what?—a gamekeeper. Sir Arnold Baxter's estate?'

'An on-site keeper, sir.'

9

'Is there a difference?'

'Oh yes, sir. The on-site keepers live in vans, sir. Out on the grounds.'

The wing commander smiled, then said, 'I know little of such subtleties, Calvert. Please explain.'

1934

Leeds was a city with a remarkably empty history. Its population was around the half-million tally. Its only real claim to fame was its size and the speed of its expansion. It was born of the wool trade, in the Middle Ages. As a stopping place on the pack trails—as a slowly growing centre of cottage industry—it prospered quietly and peacefully until the eighteenth century; until the introduction of steam-powered machinery and the arrival of the Industrial Revolution. Thereafter came mills, muck, money and a form of mass bondage as harsh as any slave relationship.

Leeds pushed out its chest, aired its muscles and became unofficial capital of the North East.

By the nineteen-thirties it boasted a whole spectrum of back-up industries to its wool-based heart; iron foundries and steel works; the manufacture of locomotives and heavy machinery; chemicals, glass, pottery, printing and leather goods. It was a railway centre; lines from the Great Northern, the Lancashire and Yorkshire, the Great Central, the Midland, the North Eastern and the London and North Western carried traffic to and from its two main stations.

Almost by definition, Leeds sprawled. It was a place of 'districts' and each 'district' nudged the city boundaries. Headingley, with its cricket ground. Holdbeck, with its workhouse. Armley, with its jail.

Each 'district' had its own character, and its own recognised place in the general pecking order of importance. Top place was out Chapel Allerton and Moor Allerton way, where the real money was, and where the toffs lived. Then came Adel and Headingley where the la-di-da folks held sway; the people who had plenty, but who never had quite as much as they made believe they had. Moortown was a few notches above Kirkstall, and Kirkstall was some distance ahead of Holdbeck. That's how it went. Woodhouse Moor wasn't so hot, but it had a slight edge on Cross Flats. And there, at the bottom of the heap—the recognised 'outlaw territory' of the city—was Hunslet.

That's where Christmas Calvert lived.

Hunslet was recognised as one of the slums of the North. Hunslet Lane sliced through the 'district'; the cobbled artery of Hunslet itself, along which rattling, swaying trams carried Hunsletites to and from the city centre.

11

Just before Hunslet Lane forked, at the Swan Junction, the 'Anchors' cut off to the right. Anchor Lane, Anchor Street, Anchor Terrace ... a dozen, or more, of them. Each was as squalid and as narrow as its neighbour. Each was as dreary. Each was as miserable. They were the very heart of Hunslet, and everything Hunslet represented.

Christmas Calvert lived in Anchor Street.

And, on this day, in 1934, at four o'clock in the afternoon, Christmas Calvert would cease to be a schoolboy. He would leave Jack Lane School for the last time, hurry home and grapple with the idea of finding a place of work in a world cursed by mass unemployment.

Caleb Calvert sponged water from the zinc bath onto his shoulders and down his back, and said, 'Seth's offer's worth thinking about.'

Hetty Calvert said, 'It would mean losing him.'

'Not *losing* him, and he'd have a trade.'

'A trade? Gamekeeping?'

Without the wrap-around pinafore, without the severe bunned hair-do and with a little make-up, Hetty Calvert would have been a remarkably attractive woman. She was slim with a good figure and a fine facial bone structure. Like her husband, she spoke with the broad vowels of Yorkshire, but without the dialect.

She reached a frying pan down from its hook above the sink in the 'sink corner' of the only

12

downstairs room of the house. She struck a match and lighted a gas ring which stood on the tiny surface alongside the sink, then she knifed a good walnut of beef dripping from an earthenware pot whose home was on a shelf in the same corner.

As she placed the dripping in the frying pan, she said, 'Fried bread for you, love?'

'Please.' Then, as an afterthought, 'And do yourself a slice. You, *and* the lad. Not just half a slice each. Damn, we can afford three slices of bread. Even *we* can afford that.'

Caleb Calvert pushed himself into an upright position from his squatting posture in the bath. His body showed the ingrained 'tattoo' marks of the underground miner. It was unnaturally white, as if it had been starved of sunlight for too long. From his right upper ribs, down and across the spine, a vicious scar was evidence of a near-fatal accident in Middleton Colliery.

As Hetty handed him a worn towel with which to dry himself, he said, 'He's not going to stand at street corners. He's a man, now. That's what the law says. If there's work available, he'll take it.'

Hetty lifted the lid of a bread tin, took out a white loaf and sliced off two slices. She cut one of the slices in two, then dropped the sliced bread into the melted dripping.

She said, 'I'll tell the truth. I've always thought your brother a bit of a hard man.'

'Seth?' Caleb sounded surprised. Almost shocked.

'He treats that dog of his like dirt.' Then, after a pause, 'And he's not much better with his wife.'

'He's strict. That's all.'

'Is that what you call it?'

Caleb finished drying himself. From a rail above the Yorkist Range he took a cotton 'union' shirt and, with the help of a collar stud, fastened it up to the neck. He rolled the sleeves of the shirt to above his elbows then, from the same rail, he took a pair of worn, and recently washed, flannel trousers and pulled them over his skinny legs.

He hefted the zinc bath and, being careful not to knock against the frying pan, poured the coal-dust-stained water down the sink. Then he picked up the towel again, and started to rub his still-damp hair.

'Put something on your feet, love,' she said.

He grunted, then said, 'He'd be in the country. He'd breathe God's good air. Not this muck.'

'I just want to be able to keep an eye on him. That's all.'

'We'll ask him.' He worked his bare feet into a pair of ancient, but comfortable carpet slippers. 'When he gets home. He's a man, now. We'll let *him* decide.'

14

'Ten shots,' mused the wing commander. 'Nine bulls and an inner. And you seemed surprised that the range sergeant made mention of the fact.'

Calvert said, 'The inner was the first shot, sir. The sighting shot.'

'The sighting shot?'

'To see how much out of true the sights on that particular rifle were.'

'Good God!'

'The rest were all bulls. Obviously.'

'Obviously?'

'There wasn't much wind, sir. Not enough to deflect the bullets.'

The wing commander stared at Calvert for a long moment or two. He seemed to be checking out the possibility that the airman might be indulging in some form of involved insolence. He flicked the bottom, right-hand corner of a form he'd taken from the folder.

Then he said, 'Let me put it this way, Calvert. I know men—men who've shot at Bisley—acknowledged, international marksmen who, had they fired ten rounds from a Lee Enfield rifle they'd never handled—never even seen—before, and amassed your score— nine bulls and an inner with the first ten shots ... they'd dine out on the incident for months.

15

For myself, I'd count it as impossible—a fluke—had you not *done* it. And, apparently, quite deliberately. Had I not double-checked with the range sergeant that you *had* done it.'

There was a silence. Calvert looked a little unnerved.

He muttered, 'I'm sorry, sir.'

'Sorry?'

'If I've done—y'know ... anything wrong.'

'I take it you're not trying to pull my leg, airman.'

'Oh!' Calvert blinked, then blurted, 'Oh no, sir. Nothing like that, sir. I—y'know—it's my *job*, sir. It *was* my job. Shooting, I mean. Just about the only thing I did. So ...'

Calvert stopped speaking. There was nothing else he could think of to say. He was at a loss as to why this senior RAF officer should have sent for him; what the interview was about; what he'd done that was so unusual.

That morning his drill sergeant had taken him aside from the squad, and told him to be on a certain promenade seat at a certain o'clock. Nothing more. No explanation. Just the simple, direct order, which had been dutifully obeyed and, as a result, he'd been contacted by a WAAF sergeant and brought to this hotel to confront this wing commander. It didn't make sense. Even in a world in which orders were blindly obeyed, regardless of the senselessness of those orders, this was ridiculous.

16

And why?

Apparently because, two days ago, he and the rest of the squad had been taken north along the coast, to the Rossall Sands, and the outdoor range looking out to sea. They'd each been given a Lee Enfield rifle, and six rounds of .303 ball ammunition. The range sergeant, and his two corporals, had carefully explained how to load, how to aim and how to fire. Then they'd all sprawled on the firing step and fired.

Calvert had lined the blade of the foresight up with the U-notch of the rearsight, taken a couple of deep breaths, brought the tip of the blade slowly up the six o'clock on the bull, and squeezed the trigger. The bullet hole had been about two inches from the bull, at ten o'clock. Thereafter, the tip of the blade had been two inches from the bull at four o'clock. Naturally.

The other nine rounds had punched a slightly widening hole in the bull. Naturally.

After the third bull, the range sergeant had stood alongside the sprawling Calvert, watched the target through binoculars and had breathed, 'Judas Christ!'

And now, this.

It didn't make too much sense, and it was a little worrying.

The wing commander returned the form to the folder. He closed the folder, then spoke.

He said, 'You pose a problem, Calvert.'

'Sir?'

'I think we should seek professional advice.'

Calvert looked perplexed.

The wing commander said, 'Wait downstairs in the entrance hall.'

'Yes, sir.'

'Sergeant Avril Morton will join you there. Have tea and biscuits ... something like that. She'll tell you what course I've decided upon.'

Christmas Calvert stood up, snapped off as smart a salute as he was able, and left the room. He descended the stairs and sat in an armchair in the hall of the hotel. He did not have tea. He did not have biscuits. Instead he sat there, feeling slightly self-conscious in his stiff, new uniform, while officers and NCOs of various rank passed him, some glancing at him with quick frowns of puzzlement and vague disapproval.

About half an hour later, the WAAF sergeant joined him.

She smiled and said, 'I have orders.'

'Oh!'

'To look after you. To keep my eye on you. Until two o'clock next Monday.'

'Why? What's...'

'St Anne's Memorial Hospital. You've an appointment with Doctor Ridgeway. Flight Lieutenant Ridgeway.'

'Why? What's...' repeated Calvert.

'My name's Morton. Sergeant Morton. But you'd better call me Avril.'

'Oh!'

'So, now let's get outside, and find

18

something amusing to do.'

They left the hotel and, two hours later, as they sauntered back to the pier-head, from the North Pier jetty, Calvert realised that he'd rarely enjoyed himself as much as he had in the company of the WAAF sergeant.

By this time they called each other Chris and Avril. By this time all differences in rank or length of service had vanished. By this time they were both remarkably at ease in the other's company.

She said, 'Right. Eating time. What do you fancy?'

'Fish and chips?' he suggested.

'And why not?'

'Only—er—Avril...' He stopped, turned to face her and looked embarrassed.

'Yes?'

'Y'see—y'know—I haven't been on a pay parade yet. I don't think I can afford two...'

'You're not going to "afford" *anything*.'

'Look, I'm not...'

'The Air Ministry, my pet. They'll foot the bill.'

'What?'

'My job,' she explained. 'Orders. See? To look after you. To deliver you, fit, sober and in good fettle to St Anne's Memorial Hospital, next Monday. That requires certain expenses ... to be met by the people in the top office.'

'Ah!'

'So-o, let's find a good, expensive fish and

19

chip restaurant and enjoy a nice, tasty blow-out.'

They found their restaurant in a street behind the Tower. They enjoyed haddock and chips, bread and butter and strong, sweet tea and, for an hour or so, the shortages of war were little more than a bad memory.

Then they made their way to the Tower. They moved slowly around the tanks in the aquarium; losing, then finding each other in the green-tinged gloom. They drank at one of the bars. They watched the dancers on the ballroom floor. They watched the cats, pacing back and forwards behind the bars in the menagerie. They had tea and cakes in one of the quick-snack cafés. Then they returned to the ballroom.

'Pity you can't dance,' she said.

'Out on the moors,' he smiled, 'you don't find too many dance floors.'

They contented themselves with watching other couples circulating and listening to the band.

As they were leaving the Tower—in the entrance hall, immediately within the blackout partition—a fight was brewing up. Half a dozen airmen were wrestling with a duo of revolvered RAF police. An over-large input of booze had made the airmen reckless, and one was wielding an already broken chair, ready to do battle with anybody silly enough to venture within range.

20

Obviously the situation was getting beyond the control of the RAF police. She held out her arm to stop Calvert from getting too near the brawl, then said, 'Stay out of it. This is my business.'

She stepped briskly forward, gave a quick nod of recognition to one of the RAF police then, while he was struggling with two of the airmen, she smoothly unholstered his revolver, stepped back as far as the lanyard would allow and, holding the gun in a two-handed grip, squeezed off two deliberate shots into the ceiling. The sound of the explosions ricocheted off the walls of the hall, magnified by the enclosed space. Everybody—airmen, RAF police and spectators—froze into momentary immobility and, in the unnatural silence after the shots, the distant sound of music from the ballroom could be heard.

Morton lowered the barrel of the revolver until it was aimed at the face of the man with the chair.

She snapped, 'Lower it, airman. Slowly, and very carefully.'

As he obeyed, she arced the snout of the gun until it stared at each of the others in turn.

'Against the wall,' she ordered. 'Hands clasped behind the neck. And don't any of you even think about trying *anything*.'

They obeyed. Some reluctantly, some in such a rush that they almost tripped over their own feet. But they all obeyed.

The onlookers looked as if they'd like to applaud.

The RAF policeman whose gun Morton was holding, finished straightening his tunic and readjusting his webbing belt, then said, 'Back-up's on the way. We've already telephoned.'

'Good.' She handed back the revolver. 'Hold them there till they arrive. And don't hesitate to shoot, if necessary. I suggest the legs, or the shoulder.' He took the gun, and she ended, 'I'll send a report in. I'll justify the Wild West tactics.'

'Thanks, sergeant.'

She glanced at Calvert and moved her head. He followed her through the blackout partition and onto the darkened prom. When he was level with her, she threaded her arm through his, and he felt the slight tremble which was the reaction to the incident.

'I could have done without that,' she murmured.

'You did fine. It was the only way.'

'I shouldn't have had to intervene. If they'd known their job, I shouldn't have had to take over.'

'Intervene?'

'What the hell else?'

'Look—I'm sorry—but what *are* you? I mean, where do you get the authority to...'

'I'm from the Provost Marshal's Office ... now, don't ask any more questions.' Her voice was brusque and sharp with authority. She

22

steered him across the prom and said, 'I need a few lungfuls of good, sea air. Let's walk on the beach for a while.'

For about fifteen minutes they walked in the gloom of the beach. The blacked-out prom, the blacked-out piers and the blacked-out traffic gave no light. Only the hint of illumination from a quarter moon and a handful of stars lighted their way through the soft, dry, heavy sand. Nobody could see them.

They coupled, as if by mutual agreement, but it was all lust and no love. He mounted her with all the hasty crudeness of a rutting stag. She tried to quieten him a little, but it was no good. He did what he wanted to do, then climbed to his feet.

She also stood up, brushed her skirt and said, 'The first ... eh?'

'What?'

'I'm the first woman you've ever had. Don't deny it. It's so obvious, it's laughable.'

'I'm sorry,' he muttered. 'I didn't mean to ...'

'Oh yes, you *did* mean, boy. You very much "meant", and the hell with anybody else.'

They walked back to the prom in silence. Then she stood, with her arms stiff and her hands clenched around the top rail, staring out to sea.

She said, 'You're billeted down by the South Shore. Right?'

'Hill Street. Off Dean Street. A couple of

streets inland.'

'Uh-huh.' She turned and rested her elbows on the top rail.

In a musing voice, she said, 'I have to keep my eye on you, so you'd better move into the place where I am. A seafront hotel, not too far from the Imperial. Move in tomorrow. I'll fix it.' Then a pause and, finally, 'Meanwhile you'd better spend the night with me. You need some basic lessons in the art of gentle, prolonged and enjoyable fornication.'

1934

To adequately describe Seth Calvert it is necessary to use contradictory terms. He was a miniature giant. He stood two inches short of six feet, and yet he gave the impression of being huge. Unlike his brother, Caleb, his skin was weather-burned to the brown of a Camberwell Beauty. He was chunky; solid; thick-limbed and short-necked. He was also unusually hairy; his head was covered by a great bush of dark bronze hair. A heavy, untrimmed moustache covered his upper lip and sprouts of the same coloured hair grew in two clumps from his high cheeks. The backs of his hands were thick with the stuff, as were his arms and his chest. Indeed, his whole body was draped in the rich, hirsute covering, like a one-piece, woolly protection.

24

He wore a heavy tweed knickerbocker suit, thick-soled brown boots and thick stockings. He smoked a pipe—a cherrywood—and, whatever the mixture was, the fumes from it filled the compartment like a faint but evil-smelling mist.

The tiny train pulled out of Pately Bridge and hauled its three carriages north towards Wath and Ramsgill.

Seth took the pipe from his mouth long enough to growl, 'Won't be long now, lad.'

'What's he like?' asked Chris.

'Who?'

'This Sir Arnold Baxter I'm going to work for.'

'Don't fret. Tha'll no'an see him too often. Tha'll be out in thi van, ten mile and more from t' big house.'

'Oh!'

And that was it, until the train pulled in at a tiny station, with a single station-master's office-cum-ticket-office-cum-enquiry-office as its only structure other than the platform. No houses could be seen. Only a hedge-lined, dirt road which ended at the loose-gravelled car park of the station. An ancient and much-abused Daimler tourer was standing in the car park.

Christmas Calvert followed his uncle from the train, from the station and to the parked car. He piled his single suitcase and brown-paper carrier onto the back seat, then followed as the older man settled himself alongside the part-uniformed driver.

The driver said, 'Have a good journey, Mester Calvert?'

Instead of answering the question Seth Calvert growled, 'Straight to my place. Then you can take t' car back to t' house. Sir Arnold'll happen be wanting it.'

Seth spoke no more to the driver, but as the car rolled majestically along the verged roads, Chris realised that the occasional remark was aimed at him. This, despite the fact that Seth never once even turned his head.

'Yon wood—atop o' yon knoll. There's a few red squirrels in there. Keep your eye on 'em. Some o' the blasted townies out on their bikes aren't above chucking stones at 'em. Lamin' 'em, sometimes.

'See that tree? That elm? It's boogered. Next fair to middlin' gale an' it'll be down. There's a badger's set just alongside, under t' hedge. It's worth watching, if nobbut to check they aren't taking eggs, or even young bird.

'Tha sees, young Chris, it's nobbut game birds we're here to fend for. Pheasant, grouse, partridge and quail. Keep *their* numbers up, an' Sir Arnold'll be satisfied. All t' rest— rabbits, hares, foxes and such like—they're best off hanging on a gibbet.'

These and other, similar remarks were made while Seth Calvert stared ahead at the winding, field-flanked road. Beyond the fields—as the

26

Pennines rose to their majestic height—the ling and bracken were punctuated here and there by outcrops of dark rock. It was Yorkshire at its wildest, and somewhere up there, among the steep-sided gullies and towering fells—somewhere lost in the fern and heather, the tumbled dry-stone walls and the solitary, wind-bent trees—Yorkshire merged with Lancashire but, other than an occasional ordinance stone, the boundary was unmarked.

Then, quite suddenly, they rounded a corner, ran alongside a six-foot-high brick wall, and came to an open gate with pillars at each side. They turned into the gate, drove along a tarmac drive for less than a hundred yards, then turned left and onto a dirt road which led through a thickening wood. Then came the cottage. Stone built, small windowed, steep roofed and tucked away in its own private shelter of holly, oak and rhododendron. The car stopped at the entrance and, from the rear, a golden cocker spaniel came busying out, tail wagging, ears flapping and tongue panting a welcome.

As he hauled himself from the car, Seth Calvert lashed out at the dog with a heavily booted foot, missed and snarled, 'Shut up, you noisy devil. Get back into thi kennel.'

The dog took little notice, other than to keep its distance.

Chris climbed out of the car, taking his meagre luggage with him and, as he rounded the corner of the cottage, he saw the gamekeeper's gibbet for the first time, and realised the significance of at least one remark of Seth's on the way from the station. The gibbet was like a small-scale goalpost and dangling from the top bar was a revolting selection of dead creatures of the wild. Two magpies, a crow, a jackdaw, two rooks, two weasels, a stoat and a grey squirrel. These and a handful of half-rotted, unidentifiable lifeless bodies, were all nailed by the neck, or the head, to the horizontal bar of the gibbet.

Seth Calvert noticed Christmas's morbid interest and said, 'That's where the boogers belong, young Chris. Keep t' gibbet well stocked. They know. They're not *that* daft. There's one by t' van. Tha can fill that one an' all.'

Before Chris could answer, the door of the cottage opened and a slim, middle-aged woman smiled a greeting. She wore her well-streaked hair in a severe, brushed-straight-back-bun-at-the-rear style. Her nose was narrow, and her upper lip was thin. Taken one at a time, she had not one feature which could be honestly called beautiful, but the whole combined to make the face look quite delightful.

She wiped damp hands on her pinafore, smiled and said, 'Christmas! It's grand to see you, lad. How are they all at Leeds?'

'Fine. They send their love.'

28

'Come inside, lad. Have a bit of a rest after your journey.'

'Not too long,' warned Seth. 'I want him out at t' van before the light goes.'

They went into the cottage. It was late afternoon, and a chill had seeped into the air. A large iron kettle was simmering on a hob, behind which blazed a fire, mainly made up of burning logs. The woman brewed strong tea, then poured the tea into pint-sized mugs, over-sweetened it and, without asking, added milk. She put the mugs on the plain, deal-topped table, alongside a cake stand piled high with home-made, buttered scones.

She said, 'Tuck in, pet. A lad your age should have a good appetite.'

'Thank you, Auntie Mabel.'

Seth Calvert sucked tea into his mouth noisily, then growled, 'Don't take too long. It's a fair way to t' van.'

'We'll get there.' Then, 'Do you go to church, Chris?'

'No.' Chris shook his head, then bit into another scone.

'That's a bit shameful. Especially with a name like yours.'

'His name's booger all to do wi' it. He didn't pick his own name, did he?'

'I say my prayers,' volunteered Chris. 'Every night.'

'On your knees?'

'Oh yes, of course.'

29

'Because God doesn't take much notice of "pillow prayers", y'know.'

'On my knees, auntie. Honest.'

Seth sniffed.

Mabel Calvert said, 'I'm staying with you tonight, Chris. To see you're all right.'

Seth growled, 'There's no need for that. He'll no'an ...'

'I'm staying with him.' Her voice was firm. 'He's our responsibility, now. I need to show him the ropes.'

'He shoots owt, bar pheasant, grouse, partridge and quail. I've told him that, already. That's all he has to learn.'

'Calvert.' She almost snapped the name out. 'You'll be with your friend, I take it?'

'I reckon.'

'Stay with him for the night ... just don't ask him here, in *my* bed.'

'I'm going.'

'You won't be missed.'

For a moment, it looked as if Seth Calvert might explode in uncontrolled anger. But his jaw muscles tightened, his face flushed, and then, with an almost conscious effort, he relaxed a little, stood up from the table and stomped out of the house.

The temporary build-up of tension was lost on Chris. He was too young to feel the change of 'atmosphere' in the room. Nor did he know either Seth or Mabel well enough to detect the change in their tone of voice.

30

Mabel said, 'When you're ready, pet. Calvert's right, there. We want to be off before it gets too dark.'

They finished their tea and scones. Mabel washed the mugs and plates, then led the way to the rear of the cottage, to where a donkey was already between the shafts of a cart. They were joined by the still-eager spaniel.

She stroked the moke's stiffened ears and said, 'This is Daisy.'

'Hello, Daisy.'

Chris climbed into the cart, and the dog scrambled up beside him.

'And that,' said Mabel, 'is Queenie.'

'A nice dog,' said Chris, as he bent to pat the spaniel's flanks.

'*My* dog,' emphasised Mabel. 'Nothing to do with Calvert. *His* dog is a black retriever.'

She took up the reins and the donkey trotted daintily forward towards the entrance gates, pulling the cart at a brisk walking pace.

The boy found the ride in the cart far more exhilarating than his previous rides on the train and in the car. The fresh smell of the countryside was pure and undiluted. The birdsong could be heard clearly, and not as a background sound. And there was a comforting feel about the gentle sway of the cart; a rhythm, as if of a peacefully rocked cradle.

They left the lane and travelled along cart tracks and bridle paths through the heather

31

and bracken—skirting steep rises and, sometimes, dropping down a gradual slope to where a rill tumbled between the foliage—and always, or so it seemed, moving farther and farther from any sign of civilised habitation.

To the right, about a hundred yards away, the evening sun glinted on the smooth surface of a stretch of water at the foot of a rock cliff.

'Blackwater Tarn,' said Mabel. 'Wigeon and Teal favour there. Moorhens and Coots. Nobody knows how deep it is. It has a bad reputation. It's wise to stay clear.'

'Why?' asked the boy.

'Things happen.' She frowned, then continued, 'Out here, pet, it's not like Leeds. Not like Hunslet. I'm not saying it's dangerous, but it's best to listen to advice from them who know. Blackwater Tarn isn't liked too much. The shooters—the poachers—steer clear. They'll take the duck ... but not over the water. The dogs won't go in.'

Daisy kept up her steady pace and, less than fifteen minutes later, they rounded a knoll and saw the van.

It was a remarkably well-built structure. The sides were of inch-thick planks, caulked like the hull of a ship, then tarred and bitumened, until it could shrug off even the weather thrown at it in this isolated spot. It had a heavy, stable door and a tiny four-quartered window, paned with glass that looked to be half-an-inch thick. The convex roof was treated much like

32

the walls, and from one end of the roof, a six-inch iron pipe, obviously a chimney, poked at the sky. The structure was on four spoked wheels with iron rims, and the boy recognised it as something usually found at the site of major road works, which necessitated the presence of a live-in watchman. The van nestled in a bower of evergreens and wild apple trees which, in turn, formed the spur of a small, elongated coppice.

A little way from the van stood an old railway van, resting on timbers to keep it clear of the ground.

The whole looked unusually welcoming, even comforting, after their journey through the wildness of the fells.

Mabel halted Daisy and climbed from the cart. Chris and the dog followed her to the door of the van and, after she'd unlocked a particularly sturdy padlock at the door, followed her inside.

It had looked cosy. It *was* cosy. There was a small table set beneath the window; a bunk bed, which stretched the width of the van; a large, slow-burning, enclosed, cast iron stove set on a base of fire brick; two cane-bottomed kitchen chairs and a battered, but comfortable-looking armchair. There were two wall cupboards, one of which held crockery and cutlery, the other of which held stacked copies of countryside and gamekeeping magazines. There was a thick-planked 'bunker' in one corner of the room which was filled with coke, coal and kindling wood. There was a wash-basin and its jug on a tiny stand.

All this at first glance, and Chris felt an immediate empathy as soon as he entered the shelter and comfort of the place.

Mabel moved towards one of the cupboards. She said, 'I trimmed the wick of the lamp yesterday. The stove's ready for a match. Half an hour should see us settled in, and I'll make some tea, when I've stabled Daisy.'

She placed a paraffin lamp on the table, scratched a match into flame, then bent and touched the waiting newspaper at the base of the stove.

Then she left the van, unharnessed Daisy and led her to the second structure—the railway wagon—opened the sliding door and revealed a well-built stall, already hayed up and waiting.

Obviously Daisy was no stranger to the place and, within half an hour, the donkey was settled in, enjoying her evening meal, having been combed and curried.

And all the time the boy watched, helped when he could and began to learn ways and skills that were completely foreign to the Hunslet wherein he had lived his life. He learned swiftly, if only because he wanted to learn. Already the feral desolation of this high country was working its magic. He 'belonged'. He was easily 'at home'. And it never entered his head to be frightened of the wilderness which stretched for miles in the thickening gloom.

*　　*　　*

It was dark, and they sat talking: the boy on one of the kitchen chairs and his aunt in the comfort of the armchair. The dampers on the stove had been balanced, and it was warm without being stifling. The lamp gave a steady, yellow wash of light, and the van was as comfortably snug as a womb.

They talked as equals, and they talked of things a little alien to the boy but, despite that, of great interest. She'd shown him the 'gun box' screwed firmly to the van's floor, under the bunk bed; she'd removed the contents, and told him their names and their purposes, before returning them to the box and turning the key, in yet another impressive-looking padlock. Now she was giving quiet advice.

'The twelve-bore. That's your working gun, Chris. Get used to it. As I've said, it's a Venere Extralusso. Italian, but don't be put off by that. It has a full Purdey-type under bolting, selective automatic ejectors ... it's as near a Purdey as doesn't matter, but not quite as expensive. Keep it clean. Always! Keep it oiled at all times. It won't let you down.'

The boy nodded, and bent to scratch the ears of the dog lying at his feet.

She said, 'The same with the four-ten Savage. It's one of the new under-and-over models. Seth doesn't find fault ... and that's a good sign. The top barrel takes two-two ball ammunition, but that's not much good for anything other than small vermin. But keep it clean and oiled, pet. Remember, it's one of the tools of your trade. Respect it, and it'll respect you.'

The boy still moved his fingers in the fur around the dog's ears. There was a small silence, then he began, 'Does Uncle Seth...'

'He's not your uncle,' she interrupted.

'Oh!'

'He's Caleb's brother ... that's all.' Then, after a pause, 'And Caleb isn't your natural father. Then, you know that already. That's what Hetty tells me.'

'She said,' muttered the boy, 'she said *you'd* tell me ... but it doesn't matter.'

'It matters, love.' There was genuine compassion in her tone. 'It matters to Hetty and Caleb. They want you to know the truth.'

'It *doesn't* matter.'

'You were found on Leeds station. Central station.' If she'd heard his half-objection she gave no sign, but her voice was quiet and caring. 'You were well wrapped up. Left on the seat in the general waiting room. The police took you to Leeds Infirmary—where Hetty was a nurse. Your natural mother couldn't be found, and Hetty claimed you as her child.

36

Nobody minded. Not in those days. And Hetty and Caleb were newly married. Like me, she was barren.' A pause, then, 'You know what that means, Chris?'

'You can't have babies,' mumbled the boy.

'That.' She nodded. 'Some people think it's a curse. That women aren't complete women, without babies. I think Hetty had views along those lines. She's wrong, of course.' A faint smile touched her lips. 'If she wasn't wrong, what does that make rabbits?'

'I'm sorry?' He looked puzzled.

'It doesn't matter, pet.' She looked sad. 'A queer sense of humour, that's all.'

He blurted, 'It's my mum and dad. That's all. All the rest is nowt.'

'You're a good son,' she said solemnly. 'Adopted, or not—whatever—you're a good son.'

There was a silence. For a few moments, no more than the time it takes to allow a red hot poker to cool, the rapport was lost. The affinity wavered. Then the boy glanced across at her, and mended the link with a slow, shy smile.

He said, 'I'm sorry, auntie. I was rude. I shouldn't have been.'

'Upset—that's all.' She smiled back.

'I'm sorry.'

'Seth should come out to see you tomorrow.' She changed the subject abruptly. 'He'll try to bully you. Don't let him. Listen to him. When it comes to shooting, trapping and the general

37

lore of the countryside, few men can equal him. But he'll try to bully. He always does. Stand up to him, Chris. Like all bullies, he's a coward at heart.'

The boy listened, but couldn't understand. How a woman could criticise her husband in this way was something beyond his comprehension. Something he had never before encountered. Nevertheless, he liked this wife of his father's brother, despite the age gap. She was, he thought, a little older than the woman he insisted upon calling Mother, but much more unorthodox. More easy to talk to. Even to disagree with.

They chatted as equals for more than an hour, then she pushed herself upright from the armchair.

She said, 'I'm going out for a while. Taking Queenie for a short walk. While I'm out, get undressed and into bed. I'll give you plenty of time.'

'I thought...' he began.

'What?'

'I thought you'd be using the bed. I'd sleep in the armchair.'

'It's your bed, Chris. I'll sleep in the armchair. You're a breadwinner now, love. Don't forget that. Don't step aside for anybody. *Anybody!*'

38

1940

St Anne's Memorial Hospital was a scowling, disagreeable-looking structure in deep red Accrington brick. It crouched, well away from the sea, in its own thicket of laurels and rhododendrons whose thick foliage was criss-crossed by narrow, tarmac paths. Whatever its capabilities, it looked unwelcoming—as if eager to inflict discomfort, and possibly pain, without much thought to the sufferer.

It was a small hospital—a 'cottage hospital' really—with three small wards, an X-ray department, an out-patients' clinic and a handful of small rooms, used as places for consultation by visiting specialists. Having been invited inside, Christmas Calvert tapped on the door of one of these rooms, then entered.

It was gloomy inside; the slatted blinds were drawn against the blazing summer sunshine. The consultant, Martin H. Ridgeway, Ph.D.— Flight Lieutenant Ridgeway for the duration of the war—was seated at a large, roll-topped desk, alongside which was a standard, leather-covered examination couch. Ridgeway moved his head in a vague gesture towards this couch and said, 'Make yourself comfortable, airman.' Then, as if as an afterthought, 'You are Aircraftman Calvert, of course?'

'Yes, sir.'

'Good.' Ridgeway nodded at the couch again and said, 'Relax, please. I merely wish to ask you some questions. Get your reactions to certain situations. Nothing more.'

With some trepidation, Calvert swung himself onto the couch, and leaned back until his head rested on the raised section.

'Comfortable?' asked Ridgeway.

'Yes, sir.'

'Be sure you are. Loosen your tie, if that helps. Loosen the belt of your tunic. But above all, relax.'

'I'm fine, sir, thank you.'

'Good.' Ridgeway consulted a flimsy on the desk, then said, '*Christmas* Calvert?'

'Yes, sir.'

'Why Christmas? Any particular reason?'

'It's when I was found, sir.'

'Found?'

'Abandoned, sir. Then found. At Christmas. That's why.'

'I see.' Ridgeway jotted a note on the flimsy, then said, 'There's no need to keep saying "sir" all the time. I accept that you acknowledge my rank. Just act as though I was a civilian doctor. That's what I am—a doctor—and I want to establish a comfortable, patient and doctor relationship. Understand?'

'Yes, sir.'

'You're nineteen years of age?'

'Yes, sir.'

40

'And your peacetime occupation?'

'Gamekeeper, sir. On Sir Arnold Baxter's estate in North Yorkshire.'

'Gamekeeper?'

'Yes, sir.'

'Were you a good gamekeeper, Calvert?'

'Nobody ever complained, sir.'

'You enjoyed your work?'

'Oh, yes. Very much.'

'In that case, why leave it?'

'Sir?'

'Why leave the job? Why join the RAF? Why not wait until you were called up?'

'Sir, there's a war on.'

'Indeed there is.'

'I wanted to do my bit.'

'By joining the RAF?'

'Eventually I want to fly, sir.'

'I see. And meanwhile?'

'Whatever I'm told to do, sir. I'll obey orders.'

Ridgeway made more jottings, then said, 'Tell me about poachers, Calvert.'

'Poachers?'

'You were a gamekeeper. I assumed you were troubled with poachers occasionally.'

'Oh, yes sir.'

'Tell me about them.'

'That was my job, sir. To keep them down.'

'Like vermin?'

'I—er—I suppose, sir.'

'Did you?'

41

'Sir?'

'Keep them down? Poachers, I mean?'

'Oh yes, sir. Me and Seth.'

'Seth?'

'Head gamekeeper. When he was around we both had a go.'

'And, when he *wasn't* around?'

'I could handle things.'

'I see.'

'I had the Mauser.'

'The Mauser?'

'The rifle, sir. From the First World War.'

'I see. What bore would that be?'

'Nine point three.'

'And this rifle. What did you use it for ... other than scaring poachers, that is?'

'Foxes, sometimes. Feral cats. Anything, really.'

'Nine point three cartridge?'

'We sometimes used point three seven five magnum ammunition. It's the same bore, but with a larger propellant.'

'You know about these things ... obviously.'

'My job, sir. My trade. Seth taught me.'

'Seth?'

'Head gamekeeper.'

'Oh!'

'Taught me how to shoot. Taught me ... if you can *see* it, you shoot it.'

'Can you indeed.' Ridgeway paused, then said, 'You seem to be very fond of this man you call Seth.'

'Head gamekeeper, sir.'

'Yes. You keep saying so. *Were* you were very fond of him?'

'He taught me. I'm grateful.'

'But not particularly fond. Is that it?'

'I admired him for his skill. He was my father's brother.'

'Your uncle?'

'No. Not really. I've said, sir. I was adopted.'

'Quite so.' Then, 'Tell me about this gun. This Mauser.'

'Sir Arnold gave it to me, sir. When I'd been with him about a year.'

'From the last war?'

'That's what he said.'

'And you believed him?'

'That's what he said, sir. Although I have a collection of gun books at the van, and Stoeger's Catalogue for 1925 advertises it, and doesn't say much, except that it's recommended for grizzly and Alaskan brown bear.'

'And you've used it in *this* country?'

'Why not, sir?'

'Calvert, I doubt if I know as much about guns as you do, but Stoeger's Catalogue only offers sporting rifles for sale. In this case, big game rifles ... I suspect.'

'Oh.'

'I therefore repeat my question. Are you telling me that you used this rifle in this country? For foxes? Cats?'

43

'I hold a firearm certificate, sir.'

'Do you, indeed.'

'Sir Arnold is Chairman of the Standing Joint Committee, and Chairman of the Bench. He had no problem in getting me a certificate.'

'I don't suppose he had.'

'Nothing illegal, sir. It was my job. Shooting.'

There was a silence while Ridgeway scribbled notes on a flimsy, alongside the file on his desk. Calvert waited patiently.

At length, Ridgeway said, 'I'm told you are a remarkable marksman.'

'I can handle guns, sir. I've handled them since I left school.'

'Professionally?'

'As a gamekeeper, sir.'

'Tell me.' Ridgeway spoke slightly slower than before. He seemed to be picking his way carefully through the words. 'Let us assume that an enemy—a Nazi, if you will—is walking down the street. You recognise him for what he is. You know he is on a mission which, if successful, will result in the deaths of some of your fellow countrymen. You have, you will appreciate, a problem. What solution can you offer?'

'Stop him,' said Calvert, without hesitation. 'Arrest him.'

'You can't. You can't reach him. Let's say you're inside a building, some storeys from the ground. For whatever reason, you can't

44

arrest him.'

'I'd warn somebody,' said Calvert. 'The police. The authority. Somebody. I'd warn them.'

'That, too, is impossible. No telephone. No time, before the man is out of your sight and lost.'

Calvert hesitated, then said, 'If I had a gun, I'd shoot him. Obviously.'

'Obviously?'

'He's an enemy. A Nazi. If I had a gun, I'd shoot him. What else?'

'Without warning?'

'Of course. If I can't get at him, he could run off if I shouted. Shoot him. Kill him, if necessary.'

'Kill him?'

'If I had any doubt at all about hitting him. Wounding him. If there was any chance of him getting away, or retaliating. Shoot him. Kill him. Why not?'

1934

The boy slept. The journey and the excitement had tired him, but it was more than that. The moorland air was strong and the bed was surprisingly comfortable. Therefore the boy slept well.

By contrast, Mabel Calvert merely cat-

45

napped. The armchair was too cramped for real snugness and, occasionally, when she awakened from her fitful sleep, she rose, stretched herself and went to the door of the van, to enjoy the pleasure of the keen night air.

In the immediate pre-dawn greyness she spotted the man crouching low against the dry stone wall, away up the slope towards Old Cote Moor. He was running in a crouched position and, obviously, keeping as much out of sight as possible. She ducked back into the van, closed the door and turned out the lamp. Then she gently awakened the boy.

'What is it?'

'Poachers,' she said. 'I spotted one of them coming down the slope. There'll be more than one. There always is.'

'Oh!'

For no good reason, they were talking in whispers.

The boy climbed from the bunk, and without being told, hurriedly pulled on trousers and a shirt over his pyjamas. The dog, sensing the slight tension in the air, whimpered a little and seemed unable to decide whether to be happy or angry.

'Quiet, Queenie,' she warned, and the dog settled a little and was content to merely watch.

While the boy dressed, she unlocked and opened the gun box. Then she lifted the Savage under-and-over from the box, checked that it was loaded, then closed and locked the box.

When the boy was fully dressed and had finished tying the laces of his boots, she handed him the gun.

'Don't use it unless you have to,' she said. 'And use the first trigger. The four-ten shot.'

'Right.' The boy's voice was restrained enough, although it held a slight hint of excitement.

'Out of the van, into the wood,' she instructed. 'They're coming down from the right. You go to the left of the wood. There's plenty of cover. But don't show yourself unless you have to. They could be scared enough to run, but they could be nasty. Just give them the chance.'

'Yes, auntie.'

'There's a holly bush over to the left. Get behind it and watch. Keep hidden, unless you think things are getting out of hand.'

'Right.'

As she opened the door for him to leave the van she said, 'Now use your own judgement, Chris. But don't try to bluff. This type of man calls every bluff there is.'

'I'll remember.'

Suppressing a quick shiver as the cool of the morning touched his skin, Chris raced to the left of the van and ducked into the cover of the coppice.

Less than fifteen minutes later, two men strolled arrogantly up to the door of the van. They both wore well-worn caps and clothes.

47

They both needed a shave. They both had that lip-curling disdain for legal niceties which marks the petty criminal. One stood a shade over six foot, the other was slightly shorter. The taller of the two carried a single-barrelled shotgun in the crook of his arm. The other carried a custom-made, poacher's catapult. Both had ancient game bags slung across a shoulder.

The man with the shotgun stopped at the door of the van and hammered it with the ball of his fist.

He called, 'We know you're in there. We've seen the light. Let's see what sort of a nanny we have to frighten this time.'

The door of the van opened, and Mabel Calvert stood framed.

'By hell!' The taller man guffawed. 'Has tha taken to sleeping out here, now, missus?'

The shorter man cackled, 'Where's Calvert, then? Lifting his shirt flap for his fancy boy?'

'If Calvert was here,' she snapped, 'you'd run a mile. As it is, you're trespassing.'

'Oh aye?'

The taller man sneered, 'Does tha want somebody to give thee what Calvert doesn't like giving thee, then?'

'You're a filthy-minded animal, Vern Sutcliffe,' she snapped. 'And I've a mind to tell your wife what sort of remarks you make to decent women.'

'We *can*,' he jibed.

48

'By God, aye.' The shorter man grinned mockingly.

'I'll not remind you again,' she said. 'You're trespassing, and I don't doubt but those bags you have are carrying things you're not entitled to.'

'Let's go inside and find out.'

The man Sutcliffe made a move as if to enter the van, and the dog growled a soft warning.

'If that bloody thing comes too near, I'll shoot the sod.'

But he stopped and before he could make another move or say anything else, Chris's voice said, 'That you won't. *And* you'll show what you have in the bags.'

Both men spun round and saw the boy; holding the Savage, with his right hand on the breech, the right finger curled at the trigger and the barrel levelled by his side, held by an extended left arm.

'Tha what!' Sutcliffe glared and made as if to shift his own shotgun from the crook of his arm.

'Don't!' warned the boy, and there was that in his voice which froze Sutcliffe in mid-movement.

Mabel took a half step back into the van, reached with her right arm, and brought the Venere shotgun from where she'd propped it behind the door.

'Hey, missus!' The shorter man looked suddenly scared.

49

'Harry Towne,' said the woman contemptuously. 'Don't think I don't know you, too. You idle, good for nothing...'

'Bugger this for a game.' Sutcliffe's temper got the better of his good sense. 'A woman and a bloody bairn. I'll not be shoved down a bloody hole with *that*.'

He dropped the shotgun from the crook of his arm to his hand and before he could bring it to bear on anything, the Savage gave a tiny, coughing crack, and Sutcliffe fell sideways, clutching his left leg. The cartridge of rook shot—little larger than a small cigarette—had peppered its load into the shin and the thigh and, already, Chris's finger had moved to the second trigger.

Mabel lined up the twelve bore and, in a cold, no-nonsense voice said, 'Home. Both of you. Leave the bags, and shift. If not, you'll need more than tweezers, iodine and bandages.'

Towne gave a quick yelp of fright, then dropped the game bag from his shoulder and scurried away, making for the path leading from the clearing.

Sutcliffe hauled himself upright, with a few hisses of pain as he put weight on his peppered leg. He made as if to reach for his fallen shotgun.

'Don't,' rapped Mabel. 'That's one gun you'll never use again.'

'By God...'

'And it's not open for discussion. On your way, Sutcliffe, before you get something more than four-ten shot in your hide.'

The man hated the boy with his eyes for a moment, then growled, 'Tha'll rue, lad. Who the hell tha is, tha'll rue. Vernon Sutcliffe doesn't take this sort o' thing without making some sod pay ... and dearly.'

1992

They were of an age, but he had aged like well-worn leather, whereas she had aged like fine and expertly stored wine. She carried herself well; well enough to peel ten to fifteen years from her true age, without the added advantage of a good skin, an amazingly trim figure and expensive clothes.

If they still hated each other, they both kept all signs of that hatred hidden. They sat at the table at the window of a sea-front café and talked like old friends.

'You've changed,' she smiled. 'Improved, I think.' A pause. Another quick but meaningless smile, then, 'Why do men grow old better than women? And without effort. The lines make a man look distinguished. They make a woman look haggard.'

'You've never looked haggard.' He sipped at his coffee.

51

'Compliments!' she mocked gently.

'I wouldn't know how.'

'That, I believe.'

Outside, the November weather had driven almost all the pedestrians off the promenade. A very occasional tram hissed and rattled its way north, or south. Now and again the wind caught the spray from the ebbing tide and tossed showers of foam into the driving sleet.

A waitress came to the table, and he ordered fresh coffee for both of them, and buttered teacakes.

'Not fish and chips,' she said gently. 'Remember?'

'I forget only what I want to forget.'

'You *do* remember?'

When he didn't answer, she went on, 'You haven't "vanished" Marie?'

'"Vanished"?' He made believe not to understand.

'The term,' she said. 'We heard it often enough. You used it often enough. The expression "to vanish" is slightly less hateful than the expression "to murder".'

'Is it?' Then, 'Would I know?'

'Yes,' she said sombrely. 'You more than anybody else.'

'Perhaps.'

'You haven't killed her, Chris. Don't lie. Not to me. You haven't vanished her.'

'Why should I lie? And why to *you*?'

'You're asking questions, instead of

52

answering them.'

'Marie is not dead,' he said flatly. 'Otherwise, Pollard wouldn't have sent you to meet me.'

'Is she safe?'

'At this moment, safer than you are. Much safer.'

'Meaning?'

'Out there.' He gave a little jerk of his head in the direction of the South Pier. 'I could have vanished *you*. No real problem. I could even have let you handle the derringer. Self protection ... in the unlikely event of anybody seeing what they shouldn't see.'

'I think,' said, musingly, 'you might be out of practice.'

He moved his shoulders in a tiny gesture. It could have meant agreement. Equally, it could have meant disagreement.

For perhaps thirty, slow-ticking seconds they stared out of the window in silence. Here and there, swathes of wet sand scarfing the prom. The flap of a loose tarpaulin slapping itself on the railings. A tattered flag, stiff in the breeze. It was a Blackpool only the residents knew and a million miles from the sweltering, gaudy, loud-laughing bawd so beloved of the wakes week revellers.

An empty 'Seagull' coach lumbered past. A council dumper, loaded with the debris of a small demolition job, chugged and spluttered north. A coastguard Land Rover sped

53

hurriedly south along the broad boulevard of the prom meant for walkers.

The waitress brought fresh coffee and teacakes.

As she stirred sugar into her coffee, she said, 'Would you do it again?'

'I doubt it.' Then, 'The chances are I wouldn't.'

'And yet, we lived high on the hog. That to its credit.'

'We were conned.' The remark carried overtones of disgust. 'You, me—all six of us—were conned by Pollard. And Pollard got the goodies. All *we* got were reputations. The wrong sort of reputations.'

'You make it sound as if we were innocents.' She still stirred the sugar. 'As if we didn't know. As if we couldn't have backed off, long before we became the Button Squad.'

'A stupid name,' he growled.

'We didn't think so at the time. As I recall, we were quite proud.'

'We were skivvies to a psychopath.'

'We obeyed orders,' she argued. 'That's all. Obeyed orders.'

'Pollard's orders.' His lip curled.

'And Dansey's. Pollard only did what Dansey told him to do.'

'Dansey.' Unbridled contempt rode the name. 'Trevor-Roper described him as an utter shit. And, in public. *And*, he was.'

'Trevor-Roper.' Her contempt almost

matched his own. 'The academic led by the nose by the fake Hitler diaries.' Then, 'Anyway, Malcolm Muggeridge has gone on record as saying Dansey was the only top-line operative in the business.'

'Some business!' he said wearily. 'Anyway, neither you nor I came into contact with Dansey. Always Pollard. Pollard was the mouthpiece. Dansey pulled the strings. He was the puppet-master. Pollard provided the appropriate puppets ... *us*.'

'We lived well,' she insisted. 'Rationing didn't touch us, and we were free agents.'

'Free?' His curled lips reflected the bitterness of his tone. 'If I hadn't taken the D'Souza woman, *I* wouldn't be free. I wouldn't be anything. Only worm-meat.'

She sipped her coffee, then very quietly said, 'That's why I'm here. Pollard wants a truce. Before it's too late. Before either you, or he, dies of old age ... his words, not mine. He wants his daughter back in circulation.' She paused, then added, 'I think he means it, Chris. I think you've licked him.'

1934

In the cold, blue light of an immediate post-dawn morning, distant Littondale looked empty and spidery-scrawled with an endless puzzle of dry-stone walls. The river Skirfare seemed to idle its way towards its junction with the Wharfe, and the impression was that this ever-rising, ever-falling landscape had not changed since it was first planted there by the gods.

Seth Calvert growled, 'Keep thi eyes skinned, lad. Tha'll nobbut get one chance ... if that. Vern Sutcliffe knows his way about these dales as well as any man. He'll be onto us afore we know it.'

The boy didn't answer. Instead he squinted his eyes up, towards High Wind Bank and Kilnsey. He thought he might have seen a slight movement up there, but wasn't sure enough to mention it.

He'd lived in the van, alone, for just over a week and, already, he knew and had begun to love the great roll of the Yorkshire Dales. Yorkshire—or was it Lancashire?—epitomised his own deep feeling of wild independence; an unhampered determination to live his life his own way. No lords and masters. No gaffers. The right and wrong of everything determined via his own personal balance ... and suspect the voiced opinions of all other men.

On this morning, he carried the Venere twin-barrelled shotgun in the crook of his arm. A mere fourteen-year-old, but big for his age and with a natural air of confidence unusual for his age.

56

He glanced at the older man, and asked in a low voice, 'Why not a shotgun? Why bring that ... and what is it?'

'A Mauser rifle, lad. German. Sir Arnold picked it up, in t' war. I reckon t' Jerries aren't good for much, but they can make guns.'

'Sir Arnold's?'

'Aye. I've borrowed it for this morn. Then we've both, see. Shotgun and rifle.'

Once more they peered out over the rising and falling land, to where the hint of hoar frost touched the ling and the sheep-cropped turf.

Seth Calvert said, 'We'll separate. Quarter of a mile apart, about. They'll come down t' valley. Nowt surer. Whoever comes. Sutcliffe, for sure, whoever's with him. Rook shot won't keep him away.'

They separated and moved down the valley. Slowly. From cover to cover. From wind-bent tree to dry-stone wall. From limestone outcrop to the shoulder of a weather-beaten bank.

The boy moved with an inbuilt, animal cunning, and his eyes swept the landscape ahead, all the time.

He spotted Towne when they were more than four hundred yards apart. Followed him carefully. Kept himself well hidden. Crouched behind walls until he could make a quick, bent-back run for nearer cover.

The boy had cut their distance from each other to barely fifty yards when they heard the shot. It was a sharp, brittle explosion. Not like

57

the thudding impact of a shotgun being fired.

Towne straightened, hesitated, then ran in the direction from which the shot had come. The boy followed, cutting even further their distance from each other.

Towne's gun was a single-barrelled twelve-bore and as he came upon the scene beyond a jutting rock outcrop, he skidded to a halt.

Sutcliffe was sprawling, face downwards, on the turf. The scarlet from his chest was already soaking into the green. Seth Calvert was holding the Mauser—still pointing at where Sutcliffe would have been standing—and the ugly expression on his face was a mixture of hatred and shock.

Then came the noise.

Towne screamed, 'You murdering sod!' and raised his shotgun.

Three simultaneous explosions ripped through the quiet of the morning. Towne let fly with his single barrel and the boy pulled both of his twin barrels at once. The boy fired a shaved second before the man and the double-spread of shot hit Towne between the shoulder blades, causing him to stumble and fall, and the single barrel to jerk up and send its shot over Seth Calvert's head.

As Towne howled and tried to haul himself to his feet, Seth Calvert stepped nearer, tilted the Mauser and sent a round in behind the injured man's ear.

'That's two boogers less,' growled Seth.

Chris, who had never before witnessed sudden and violent death, merely watched, stony faced. As far as outward appearances were concerned, he was quite unmoved.

'Now,' said Seth, 'We'll have to shift 'em.' He nodded towards a group of weather-bent trees standing in a nest of half-dead bracken and bramble. 'There's good enough, till I get transport here.'

Seth leaned the Mauser against the rock outcrop, bent and tucked the dead Sutcliffe's feet under his arms, then hauled the corpse towards the trees. Chris did the same with Towne's body.

Blood was on the grass, and two trails of red led to the copse, but the forecast was for prolonged downpours, and anyway, no path came within sighting distance of the interior of the tiny wood.

* * *

By early light next morning, Chris Calvert had moved no short way from being a boy to being a man. He had spoken little but he had obeyed the instructions given by Seth, without argument and without hesitation.

'Wait at t' van. I'll pick you up.' Then, handing the Mauser to the boy, 'And take this. Put it in t' gun box for t' time being. We'll decide what, later.'

Seth had gone back to the house;

presumably to his own cottage. The boy had waited in the van. Patiently and without panic. He'd brewed himself tea and was glancing through a country magazine when Seth reappeared, driving an old and slightly dented Ford van.

Seth said, 'We use it at t' shoots. To get t' beaters round t' back o' t' birds.'

They travelled to the murder scene in the van, then humped the stiffening bodies into the back of the van and threw the two guns in with them.

Thereafter, Seth drove grimly but carefully. North, along the upper reaches of the Pennines. Out of Yorkshire and into Durham. To country even wilder than that where the van was parked. Along little more than mountain tracks winding their way up impossibly steep-sided slopes.

They stopped at a place more desolate than the boy had even imagined.

'Buttertubs,' explains Seth bluntly. 'Summat to do with t' underground caving system. I tell thi, lad. Many a dead sheep's been dumped down these places.'

They were like ling-hidden, bottomless wells, not far from the road. Wide enough to take a man. Deep enough for him never to be found.

By the time they left the Buttertubs, the rain was coming down like the start of the Second Flood. Nor was the cab of the van waterproof and, in no time at all, they were both soaked to the skin.

Seth parked at Bowes, and they visited a cheap café for an early evening snack. Then the man left the boy in the cab of the parked van and sought a nearby hostelry for liquid refreshment. It was almost ten o'clock when Seth returned. The boy was cold and miserable, and the man was worse for booze.

The journey back to the parked caravan was wild, wet and full of obscenities aimed at the few other road-users who threatened to stray into the path of the erratically driven Ford.

Back at the caravan, Seth wasted no time. He bundled Chris from the cab and jerked the van onto its final leg for home.

Left to himself, the boy flung himself, fully clothed, onto the bunk bed and cried himself to sleep. He had not wept for years; the folk from Hunslet didn't weep. And yet, *he* wept. Not because he was cold. Not because he was hungry. Not because he was tired. Indeed, he was all these things, and more ... but he wept because he was far too alone and without any form of guidance. He was having to reach decisions far in advance of his years, and the decisions were very frightening ones.

Therefore, he wept himself into a troubled sleep.

Ridgeway was startled by the young airman he was interviewing. As a medic—as one of a handful of leading psychiatrists who had put on uniform—he had questioned and probed sick and twisted minds, as a profession. But the mind of Christmas Calvert was not sick or twisted. It was alert. It was honest. It was everything a young mind should be ... but, at a guess, it was remarkably amoral.

Flight Lieutenant Ridgeway was, therefore, fascinated by this teenage airman.

He said, 'You are, of course, a volunteer. You weren't called up?'

'Oh no, sir. I volunteered. I needed my father's permission.'

'Why?' asked Ridgeway.

'I'm only nineteen, sir. I couldn't have...'

'No. I mean why *did* you volunteer?'

'There's a...' Calvert stared, then said, 'There's a war on, sir.'

'That won't do.' Ridgeway shook his head.

'Sir?'

'That's too pat, Calvert. It means nothing.' A pause, then, 'Let's take it a step at a time. National Socialism. Does it mean much to you?'

'No, sir.'

'Do you understand it?'

62

'Not a lot, sir.'

'What Hitler is doing—has done—for Germany. How do you view that?'

'They voted him into power, sir. It's *their* business.'

'Quite. Let's take Poland. Do you like the Poles, as a race?'

'I don't know them, sir. I don't know any Poles.'

'So, what Hitler and his generals have done to the Polish people hasn't much to do with you joining up?'

'Not a lot, sir.'

'At least you're honest.' Ridgeway smiled. 'Tell me, then, is there any one person who, figuratively speaking, you are defending?'

'No, sir. I don't think so, sir.'

'The king?'

Calvert hesitated, then said, 'No, sir. I don't think so. *I* can't defend the king, whatever happens.'

'The flag?'

'No, sir.'

'The British way of life?'

'I—er—I don't quite understand, sir.'

'The country? That's what they called it in the last war.'

'No, sir. Not that. It's too vague.'

Ridgeway rubbed the side of his jaw meditatively, then said, 'Not the Navy. You didn't decide on the Navy?'

'I can't swim, sir.'

'You can't fly, either ... but we'll let that pass. Not the Army, then?'

'No, sir. As I see things very few soldiers come face-to-face with the enemy.'

'But airmen do?'

'The flyers do, sir.'

'Put bluntly, then—you want to kill Germans?'

'Yes, sir.' Calvert nodded.

The simple, no-nonsense affirmative was so obviously the truth that Ridgeway blinked. Then he moved his attention to the slim file in front of him, and made notes in a typical doctor's scrawl.

Christmas Calvert watched the note-making, but couldn't read the scrawl. He didn't try too much. In truth, he didn't much care, and was starting to be bored with the whole business.

Then Ridgeway looked up and said, 'An adopted child. Is that right?'

'Me?'

'Yes.'

'That's what I've been told, sir.'

'Have you any idea who your real parents are?'

'No, sir. I don't want to know. I'm happy as I am.'

'Happy?'

'It isn't important. That's what I mean.'

'And...' Ridgeway glanced at the file. 'You're a gamekeeper on the estate of Sir

Arnold Baxter?'

'Yes, sir.'

'Very young,' observed Ridgeway. 'Nineteen. That's *very* young ... surely?'

'I was an on-site keeper.'

'And that means?'

'I wasn't near the hall, sir. I was out on the estate. On the moors. In a van.'

'A van?'

'A caravan.'

'Alone? You lived alone?'

'I had Queenie, my dog.'

'Just you and a dog?'

'Nobody else was needed, sir. The head keeper visited every few days. I enjoyed it. It was a good life.'

'The head keeper?'

'And his wife, Aunt Mabel.'

'Ah! The head keeper was your uncle?'

'No, sir. My father's brother.'

'In that case, he must be...'

'I was adopted, sir. I told you.'

Ridgeway sensed Calvert's increasing impatience. It wouldn't do to hurry things too much. What Ridgeway was probing for— trying to understand—was something well beyond mere personal opinion. Something deeply enough hidden to be unknown even to Calvert himself. Something as natural, and as peculiar to Calvert as his pulse rate or his normal blood pressure. Something as uncontrollable.

65

Mabel Calvert poured boiling water from the heavy iron kettle into the brown earthenware teapot, then returned the kettle to its place on top of the slow-combustion stove.

She said, 'They'll be here any minute. Calvert's meeting him at the cottage. I think they'll come in the van.'

'What does he want?' asked Chris.

'Sutcliffe and Towne.' She stirred the contents of the teapot. 'They haven't been seen for nearly a week. Their families are getting a bit worried. That's what Bobby Hargreaves told us last night.'

'Oh!'

'Sergeant Rushton wants to interview you. Calvert's arranged to bring him out.'

'Why me?'

'Chris,' she smiled, 'You peppered him with bird shot, just over a week back. His missus knows. She's told the police. They have their job to do. That's all. That's why *I'm* here. I know what happened. They won't be able to say what *didn't* happen ... see.'

Chris concentrated on straightening the clothes on his bed, then sat on a chair and began to pull his boots onto his stockinged feet.

Mabel had arrived about an hour earlier.

She'd fixed a bran-bag over Daisy's head then, accompanied by the spaniel, Queenie, had entered the caravan after a perfunctory knock on the door. She'd carried the shopping basket of food she'd brought to the table and had spent the first few minutes stacking it carefully into the wall food cupboard while Chris, stripped to the waist, had finished his ablutions via the tin bowl and cold water. She'd poured fresh water from the store jug into the kettle, then set the kettle back onto the top of the stove.

Only then had she spoken.

'The door was only on the latch. It wasn't on the bolt.'

'I know. I forgot.'

'*Don't* forget. It could save you a lot of bother.'

'Who knows about this place? Who *knows*?'

'You'd be surprised, Chris. Workmen from the hall. They all know ... and some of them aren't all they should be. Poachers. Just about everybody who lives in these parts. You're a bit isolated, lad, but you're not *hidden*. People know the van's here. It's been here a long time.'

'Sorry.' He'd pulled a heavy shirt over his head. 'I'll try to remember.'

Then she'd broken the news that the local policeman had called at the gamekeeper's cottage the previous evening, to make an appointment for the section sergeant, Sergeant Rushton, to interview Chris.

67

Chris took the bowl of dirty water out of the van and threw it against the roots of a wild rose which made up part of the back-cloth of shrubbery about ten yards from the door. He returned and began to help Mabel tidy up the van before the arrival of the visitors.

Less than fifteen minutes later the spluttering Ford drew to a halt outside and Seth Calvert and Sergeant Rushton climbed down from the cab.

Rushton was a man of his age, of his profession and of his kind. A naturally bulky body was made to look slightly ridiculous by a tight-fitting uniform and a 'choker' collar that threatened to strangle him. He had an air of pomposity calculated to make him look stupid in any moderately relaxed company.

He hoisted himself into the van then asked of nobody in particular, 'Is this the young boy, then?'

'Yes.' Mabel answered the question.

Rushton drew himself up to his full height and full girth. He hooked his left thumb through his tunic belt and beckoned with his right forefinger. It was a most imperious gesture.

Chris stepped a couple of paces nearer.

'I am told, on good authority, that you have broken the law.'

Chris looked first at Seth, then at Mabel, but said nothing.

'Well?' demanded Rushton.

'I don't know what you mean.'

'I mean, lad, that you have fired a gun into the legs of one Vernon Walter Sutcliffe.'

'More into his backside,' murmured Mabel.

'Let the lad answer for himself,' growled Rushton.

Chris said, 'He was trespassing. *And* poaching. *And* he was threatening Aunt Mabel.'

'That's not what I hear.'

'It's the truth.'

Mabel rapped, 'Whatever you "hear", Walter Rushton, the boy's telling the truth. I was here when it happened.'

'He has not been seen since,' said Rushton, still speaking directly to Chris. 'He is what is known, officially, as "Missing From Home". He hasn't been seen since you shot him. Not him nor his friend, Henry Towne.'

'And *that's* a lie,' interrupted Mabel. 'I've seen Maisy Sutcliffe. Spoken to her. She'd a lot to say for herself about her husband being peppered with bird shot. Too much to say, till I stopped her chatter.'

'I didn't kill him ... if that's what you're getting at,' said Chris.

Perhaps a little too quickly Seth Calvert said, 'Nobody's saying he's dead, lad. He's just missing.'

'He's Missing From Home,' said Rushton heavily. Then, 'It's against the law, lad, to shoot anybody with a shotgun. I could arrest

69

you. I could put you up in front of a magistrate. You could be sent to prison.'

'He's an on-site gamekeeper, sergeant,' said Seth. 'It's his job. To shift poachers.'

'Not to *shoot* them.'

'He was threatening Aunt Mabel,' repeated Chris.

'I had a gun,' snapped Mabel. 'And it wasn't a toy—it was a twelve-bore. And I'd have pulled the trigger if he'd come a step nearer. And it wouldn't have been his legs. I'd have blown his head off.' She managed a quick humourless smile. 'The lad saved his life. That's what it boils down to.'

'Missus, I am not here to argue with *you*.' Rushton scowled. 'If you go round shooting people in the head with a twelve-bore, you'll hang, nothing surer.' He turned to Chris and added, 'Now then, lad. Let's have the gun you shot Sutcliffe with.'

Chris went to the gun box and took out the Savage. He handed the weapon to the police sergeant.

Rushton carefully and deliberately examined the two breeches, to check that it was unloaded.

'A very dangerous weapon,' he proclaimed.

'Yes, sir.'

'Not to be left in the hands of irresponsible schoolboys.'

'No, sir.'

'He's not a schoolboy.' Mabel moved in

again. 'Nor is he irresponsible. He's an employee of Sir Arnold ... and *he's* Chairman of the Standing Joint Committee. Have you forgotten that?'

'Missus,' said Rushton solemnly, 'are you suggesting that I might be intimidated in some way?'

'Your superintendent is,' said Seth. 'And your chief constable. It doesn't matter much of a damn about *you*.'

'Careful, Calvert,' warned Rushton. 'You've gone far enough.'

'And *you*,' snarled Seth, 'have gone a bloody sight too far. Two ragged-arsed poachers! Mooching around looting Sir Arnold's game. And you're taking their side, against a lad who was doing his job ... and doing a good job.'

'I'm not saying anything about...'

'I reckon,' contributed Mabel, 'you'd be better employed asking that top-heavy barmaid at the Cock and Bottle. Ask her to turn down her bedclothes. You'll maybe find Sutcliffe there.'

'I have a job to do.' Rushton sounded much deflated. 'We have to examine every possibility. That's all.'

'Right.' Mabel made the word sound very final. 'I was going to offer you a cup of tea, but I won't bother. You've done your job—the job you came to do—the one you *had* to do. You can go now, and leave us in peace.'

71

Brooks's Club in St James's Street was one of the most exclusive private clubs in the capital. In the world. Most of its members were military types and, already, battles and skirmishes had been planned and abandoned within its walls.

In a corner of the club library two men sat at a table and talked in low voices. They both wore civilian clothes. One of the men was Flight Lieutenant Ridgeway. The other was, to give him his full and proper title, Lieutenant-Colonel Sir Claude Edward Marjoribanks Dansey, Knight Commander of the Order of St Michael and St George, Commander of the *Légion d'Honneur* of France, Chevalier of the *Ordre Léopold* of Belgium, Officer of the Legion of Merit of the United States of America.

Quite a man. One of the boss men in both MI5 and MI6, plus the big white chief of a handful of splinter organisations which did not officially exist. Arguably the most influential man in England, in that he not only had the ear of every member of the War Cabinet, but also had immediate, personal access to the Sovereign, if necessary.

And yet, not a very impressive man to look at. Receding hair; a cavalry officer's moustache; slightly protruding eyes behind thin-rimmed spectacles. White shirt, dark suit, quiet, single-coloured tie. A high cleric, perhaps. A headmaster. Most assuredly not a man with power of life and death, as far as the secret enemies of his country were concerned.

And yet, he had that power and for years had wielded it, without mercy and without giving it too much thought.

He said, 'You've interrogated him, Ridgeway.'

'For more than ten hours, all told.'

'You know what I'm after. You were told what to look for.'

'Yes, sir.'

'Well, then!' The eyes seemed to protrude a little farther. 'Don't pussyfoot around, man. What's your considered opinion?'

'Sir, I'd rather...'

'Damn it, Ridgeway, I don't want anything in black and white. That's why you're here. Just tell me, then fix yourself up with a seat at the Windmill. Forget you ever made the journey.'

'He might,' said Ridgeway, hesitantly.

'Might? Only *might*?'

'I—er—I think he would ... given the right training. I think the basic material's there.'

'I'll see he gets the training,' grunted Dansey. 'That's my side of things.'

'Er ... just one thing.' Ridgeway looked worried.

73

'Well?'

'There's a girl. A WAAF sergeant. He seems to be smitten.'

'Good God!'

'Besotted.' Then, after a pause, 'You'd be wise not to ignore her, sir. In the—the circumstance.'

1992

'Only the two of us left,' he said. 'Half a century ago. Six highly trained assassins. Killers. Murderers. And now, just you and me.'

'And Pollard,' she added. 'One must never forget Pollard.'

'Pollard was never one of us.' Then, 'Did *you* count Pollard as one of us?'

'No. Not really,' she admitted.

'The complete psychopath.'

'Weren't we all?'

'No!' The denial was both angry and urgent. 'We killed because we were told to kill. Some bastard pressed a button ... somewhere. We obeyed orders. We "vanished" them.'

'A stupid, childish expression.'

'We obeyed orders.'

'And that,' she said contemptuously, 'was the excuse offered by every Death Camp commandant in the Third Reich.'

They were walking slowly down the South

74

Pier. The wind and rain slashed at them, but they leaned into the weather and talked in a volume loud enough to be heard by the other. Once she made a move to link arms, but he pulled away and she smiled a little sadly. The oak planks of the pier deck were wet and slippery, and the paintwork on the shelters and pavilions were peeled and scoured. A poster showed a toothy comedian grinning out at the world, and a notice warned '*Do Not Come If You Are Easily Offended*'.

'Dirty comics,' he growled. 'Humour isn't humour these days, unless it's offensive.'

'It brings the audiences in.'

'Lavatorial,' he said contemptuously. 'The natural functions of the body . . . something to laugh at. We are an offensive breed.'

'In the old days. You weren't so prudish then.'

'I was never obscene.'

'No.' She raised an eyebrow. 'Pornographic is a more accurate description.'

'You taught me,' he murmured.

'You were an eager pupil, as I remember.'

'Perhaps.' They'd reached the end of the pier. They stopped and gazed out to sea. 'Presumably you didn't set up this meeting solely for us to build up filthy mental pictures.'

Without turning her head, she said, 'Pollard's an old man, Chris.'

'*I'm* an old man.'

'You know what I mean.'

'No. Tell me.'

'There's some doubt about whether he'll last the year out.'

'It's little more than a month to Christmas and New Year.'

'It's *that* close.'

'And?'

'He wants to see his daughter. For the last time.'

'And you believe him?' he asked mockingly.

'I believe the specialists. Two of them. They both say the same. His life can be counted in days. Weeks at the most.'

'Good.'

'For God's sake!' She sounded both shocked and angry. 'He is *dying*. And knows it. It's a last request—the condemned man's last request, if you want to put it that way—even uncivilised peoples grant *that*.'

'As I recall, *we* didn't. We didn't even tell the poor bastards they were condemned.'

1935

Seth Calvert sucked his yard-broom moustache noisily. It was an outward sign that he was thinking. He stared out over the ling-covered undulations and hugged the Mauser rifle tight in the crook of his right arm. The left sleeve of his jacket was hanging empty; the arm

76

was well bandaged and held in a soiled triangular sling.

'See owt?' he growled.

'Nothing so far.' Chris held binoculars to his eyes and swept the landscape.

'The boogers are out there,' said Seth. 'Two bloody dogs running wild. They've been seen too often. Alsatians ... so the hill farmers tell me. Bad as bloody wolves, they are. Sheep. Lambs. They'll be after *our* stock next.'

'No.' Chris swung the binoculars from left to right before he lowered them.

'Damn townies,' grumbled Seth. 'They bring their bloody animals out here. They can't control the flaming things. An' next thing you know there's sheep worrying, dead lambs and sporting stock chased to hell and back. I'd shoot them, *and* their bloody dogs if I had my way.'

Thereafter there was a silence of about three minutes; a silence made more absolute by the distant weeping of a curlew, the nearer chirp of a plover and the steady, quiet moan of a breeze that was never far from the high tops.

And yet, and despite his upbringing, Christmas Calvert loved and was part of that magnificent solitude. He'd lived in the van, alone, throughout the winter and had never once felt lonely. Seth had visited him about twice a week, Mabel slightly less often. Alone he'd explored his untamed kingdom; tramped around the edge of Blackwater Tarn; tramped

77

Old Cotes Moor; watched the tiny wildlife on the banks of the Wharfe. And always with his Venere, or his Savage, tucked under an arm, loaded and ready for use.

He'd shot rabbits and, once, a marauding fox. He'd aimed and squeezed at various inanimate targets—a few rounds each day— and gradually he'd become more and more proficient in the handling of a gun. Seth had given him basic guidelines—'Don't jerk t' bloody trigger—don't even pull—just squeeze—t' gun'll do t' rest,'—or, 'Pull it into thi shoulder, lad. Hard. The harder tha pulls it in the less t' kick'—but he'd soon realised that he was a natural shot. The lining up of the sights when necessary. The swing of the barrel with the movement of the target. The smooth kiss of the stock against his cheek. The thrill of hitting exactly what he was aiming at.

Two days ago Mabel had called at the van with the news that Seth had fallen and broken his wrist. Without saying so, she'd left little doubt that booze had been the reason for his fall.

Yet, despite that, this morning Seth had shown up at the van, had insisted upon loading the Mauser and had led the way into the wilderness in search of the reported dogs.

'How's tha getting on out here?' asked Seth quietly, conversationally.

'Fine.'

'Sorry tha came?'

'No. Glad, actually. I like the life.'

'Tha'd a quiet Yuletide, I reckon.'

'I read a lot. I don't like parties and such.'

'Aye.' Seth nodded his approval. 'Like me. Let them silly boogers as want make fools o' themselves. Summat warm in thi belly, that's all anybody *really* needs.'

And indeed it had been so. Over the end-of-the-year period Mabel herself had either called each day, or had sent one of the estate workers out to visit. She'd either brought, or sent, home-made pies to warm up. Chicken. Rabbit. Pork. Veal. A bottle of elderberry wine, from earlier in the year. But most important of all, as it turned out, a collection of books with which to while away the dark evenings.

The choice had been hers, and it had been a clever choice. Edgar Rice Burroughs: *Tarzan of the Apes*, *The Return of Tarzan* and *The Son of Tarzan*. Henry Rider Haggard: *King Solomon's Mines, Allan Quatermain* and *Montezuma's Daughter*. John Buchan: *The Thirty-Nine Steps, Greenmantle* and *Prester John*.

Less than a dozen books. None of them hard reading. Each a yarn of wildlife and adventure. Yet by the time he'd read them, Christmas Calvert was hooked for life. He could recognise tat and appreciate good story-telling. Eventually and in time, he would recognise literary excellence.

Perhaps because of his reading skill—

79

certainly because of his shooting skill—Seth had begun to treat him almost as an equal. Seth was still boss, but Chris was no lackey. Nor was it unimportant that the boy, although still not quite fifteen, topped the man by a good inch and weighed all of eleven stone, without a trace of surplus fat.

Seth said, 'Tha'll have to keep thi eyes open when tha's making thi rounds. The boogers will no'an...'

'There!' Chris pointed to a wall, all of three hundred yards to their front; to a gateless gap, and movement deep in the wall's fern-covered base.

'By God.' Seth squinted at the spot then added, 'Tha's good eyesight, lad.' He dropped the Mauser into his right hand and held it out. 'Try a kneeling shot. And aim for t' shoulder. If it doesn't kill, it'll cripple, and the bastard won't be able to go far with a main bone smashed.'

Chris took the rifle and dropped onto his left knee. Without being told, he adjusted the sight slightly, put a round into the breech and cuddled the stock to his right cheek.

'Steady,' warned Seth in a whisper. 'Tha'll not get a second shot. Just get...'

The explosion of the Mauser being fired cut him off in mid-sentence.

'Damn!' Then, '*Damn*! By God, that's got t' booger.'

The dog seemed to catapult its body off the

80

ground, then return to earth as if all its bones had suddenly melted. The second dog came into view. A quick sniff at its fallen companion, then it turned and raced for safety.

Without taking the Mauser from his shoulder, Chris slammed a second round into the breech, steadied his aim for a split second, then fired again.

The second dog cartwheeled, tried to get to its feet, failed and sprawled on the turf.

For a moment Seth was speechless, then he gave a great roar of approval and yelled, 'Both the sods. *And* a running target. By God, if tha meant it—if it wasn't a fluke...'

'It wasn't a fluke.' Chris pushed himself upright and held the Mauser toward Seth. 'It shoots a shade low. That's all. For me, that is. It might be perfect for you.'

The remark was made without brag—without bluster—a quiet, conversational utterance that left Seth inarticulate. A man used to boasting and exaggeration, and here was a youth—little more than a boy—capable of performing the near-impossible with a rifle but, or so it seemed, unable to comprehend that what he had done *was* near-impossible.

They walked in silence to the dead dogs. On the way they had to climb two dry-stone walls and every inch of the way was up a moderate incline. The first dog had died instantaneously; the bullet had smashed the shoulder bone, ripped its way through the heart and exited via

81

a hole not much smaller than a small cup at the base of the neck. The second dog might not have died so swiftly; the bullet had entered at an angle in the flank, torn major blood vessels apart and, like the first dog, exited via a hole above the right shoulder. Both animals were dead, with that wicked, toothy grin peculiar to all dogs meeting a sudden and violent death.

Chris stooped and grabbed the bodies by a hind leg, and he and Seth returned the way they had come. They took their time returning to the van, then Chris heaved the corpses into the back of the Ford and Seth climbed into the cab and, one-handed, and with some difficulty, started off for his own cottage.

It was only shortly after mid-morning. Mabel had sent cold beef sandwiches and home-made cake with Seth, therefore Chris brewed tea and enjoyed a meal before he left the van for an afternoon patrol of the area. He carried the Savage and gradually made his way towards Blackwater Tarn.

At the tarn—across the stretch of dark, brooding water—in sheltered cover at the base of the rock, a gypsy caravan was parked on the shingle. The green canvas was tight across the hoops; the end and the wooden sides were gaudily painted in green and red patterns. The shafts were empty and a skewbald pony nibbled close-cropped grass beyond the shingle beach. Two lurcher dogs sprawled between the front wheels of the caravan. A fire had been lighted, with an iron tripod and a hanging cauldron. A man was sitting on the shaft of the wagon, peeling the bark from a branch with an ugly-looking knife.

Chris walked around the tarn without hurry and, apparently, without sign of annoyance at the trespassers. The man on the shaft made no sign of seeing the approaching Chris, other than tossing the branch into the fire and returning the knife to its sheath. One of the dogs stood up and stretched itself. The tiny door of the caravan opened and a woman came out and squatted on the driving step.

When he was ten yards away Chris called, 'Good afternoon.'

'Young sir.' The man looked up, dark-eyed and expressionless.

'You weren't here two days ago,' said Chris.

'That, not.'

'Where are you making for?'

'Somewhere.'

'When?'

'Sometime.'

'Not too long, I hope,' said Chris.

'Maybe.'

'Two days. Three days.'

'Maybe.'

'I'm not asking.'

'No?' The man's lips twitched in a quick, quirky smile.

'Telling.'

'Can you?'

'Believe me.'

'Why should I?'

Casually, as indifferently as he might brush a speck of dust from his sleeve, Chris dropped the Savage into his right hand. With equal, unhurried ease he gripped the barrel and slipped a round into the breech. There was nothing overtly threatening in the way his forefinger curled around the trigger.

He murmured, 'Already this morning, I've shot two dogs.'

'I heard.'

'The shots?'

'It carries.'

'I could make it three. Even four.'

'I defend mine.' Equally, the words were even and not openly menacing, but the man stood up from shaft and, in the same fluid movement, unsheathed the knife and held it with the thumb on the flat of the blade.

'Stop it!' The woman spoke for the first time as she jumped down from the driving step. She walked until she was between the two, then she stopped and spoke to the man with the knife. 'Jared, we have a guest. What manners are these?'

'We're not diddies.' The man spoke as if in simple explanation. 'Romany. Not to be hounded. Hunted. Not travellers.'

'Understood.' Chris nodded. He lowered the stock of the Savage onto the ground, but neither unloaded the breech nor thumbed on

84

the safety catch.

The woman said, 'Offer our guest tea, Jared.'

She returned to the caravan, opened a tiny cupboard in the side of the vehicle and took three remarkably dainty bowls out; almost nursery crockery, except that they were of obviously fine porcelain with beautiful miniature rural scenes on the sides. She handed two of the bowls to the man and kept one herself.

The man looked at Chris and said, 'Tea?' He added, 'Root tea. Romany tea.'

'Please.' Chris nodded.

The man stepped nearer to the fire, picked up a small ladle and part-filled the two bowls before handing one to Chris. Then he passed the ladle to the woman who spooned some of the liquid into her own bowl.

They each raised their bowl before sipping, as if in some secret, silent toast.

* * *

Years later, Chris could still not explain. The mystery of friendship; the friendship of a man for a man, a man for a woman, a woman for another woman. Nothing carnal. Nothing sexual. Pure, pristine friendship. The friendship of an untamed man of nature for a boy/man from the urban slums of a city.

Just that it was there. That the mutual toast

85

of root tea sealed the pact. Each had pride. He understood and respected the other's pride.

That first day, Chris stayed at the caravan for almost two hours. They drank root tea and exchanged short sentences of conversation, and that was enough.

As he made a move to leave, Chris said, 'Stay. If that's what you want.'

'If it's what I want,' replied Jared.

'Tomorrow? Shall I see you?'

'We'll be here.'

'Good. I'll see you.'

And, with real, but confused reluctance, Chris tucked the Savage under his arm and made his way to his own van.

1941

Christmas Calvert stood at the third-floor bedroom window and gazed out at the immediate post-dawn scene. The great curve of Glen Goy took the eye up to a grey and heavy sky. The ranks of pine stood, regimentally straight, up the hillside. The scarves of mist hid the lower branches of the trees. The snow and dew frost created a world of sparkling white.

It was the sort of scene beloved by Victorian landscape artists, and Christmas Calvert approved of what he saw.

He was quite naked and the grey light

reflected on the thin film of perspiration, and made his body shine.

From the bed Avril Morton complained, 'Always in too much of a hurry. Why on earth can't you exercise more control?'

'It could be said that I'm a passionate man.'

'It could be said you're a lascivious bastard.'

'True.'

Even with his back towards her, Avril Morton knew that he was grinning. It was in the tone. The thought flashed through her mind; what a difference between Chris Calvert now, and the Chris Calvert she'd first met, some few months ago, near the South Pier. The present assurance as opposed to the previous uncertainty.

As if to underline that difference, he growled, 'What in hell are we doing here?'

'We obey orders. That's the name of the game.'

'Goy Castle? Loch Goy? What the hell *are* we doing here?'

'Ask Pollard.'

'Pollard?' He turned to face her.

'If you'd checked the notice-board when we arrived, you'd have seen. First Session. Nine o'clock. Introduction and briefing by Sergeant Instructor Pollard.'

'I am,' said Chris, 'pig sick of "Sergeant Instructors". All of them. They've already run us ragged, up and down every hill in Wales. Had us traipsing up the Pennine Way in full pack. Then traipsing down again. Over obstacle courses calculated to kill an elephant. And now, *here*. What the hell for?'

'We're very fit.'

'I was fit before I started.'

'Some weren't.'

'Four never will be,' he growled grimly. 'They've killed one and crippled the other three. What, in God's name, are they trying to prove?'

She sat up in bed, threw the bedclothes aside and said, 'You'd better go back to your room. We don't want to start by outraging the natives.' She swung her feet onto the lino-covered floor, reached to a nearby chair for a terry-gown and said, 'I'm going for a shower. I'll meet you downstairs at breakfast.'

*   *   *

Lecture Room 13b was a single-roomed wooden hut—walls, roofs, a door and four windows—with a tiny stage at one end. The body of the room contained six desks and six chairs. On the stage was an easeled blackboard and, as if to make up the set, a chair similar to the ones in the body of the room.

The hut stood alone behind a high, link-wire fence, on the edge of the pine trees, a full two hundred yards from the forecourt of the castle. At the gate of the fence, a large, scarlet-printed notice warned, '*No Unauthorised Person*

Admitted'.

The four men and two women sat at the desk. Each showed a degree of anticipation. Perhaps even the hint of worry.

On the stage a man stood motionless. Waiting. He had the build of a light heavyweight; the square-shouldered, natural aggressive stance of Freddie Mills. The hint of a broken nose. A cat-like smoothness as he paced backwards and forwards across the apron of the tiny stage. He wore RAF uniform with gleaming white, sergeant's chevrons on each sleeve. The uniform fitted perfectly— individually tailored, at a guess—and the material was smooth, officer's uniform material. His shirt was white, as opposed to the normal standard blue. His shoes shone like black glass.

He paused in his pacing, turned and addressed the six waiting members of the assembly.

'Two minutes from now. Exactly! The door will open and Colonel Dansey will enter this room. You will all jump to attention. Fast! I'll chop the colonel a salute of greeting. You lot will remain at attention until *he* decides whether or not you can relax.'

Six pairs of eyes moved upwards to watch the electric clock above the platform. The second hand ticked by. As the hand flicked upright, the door of the hut opened, a military policeman held it wide and the immaculately dressed figure of a cavalry officer marched briskly to the stage.

The sergeant slammed the officer a perfect salute and barked, 'Ready and waiting, sir.'

The six occupants of the desks shot upright and stood rigidly at attention. There was no preamble. The cavalry officer bounced onto the stage, turned to face the audience of half a dozen and spoke in a brisk, no-nonsense voice.

'My name's Dansey. Colonel Dansey. I am the only officer you are answerable to. The only officer authorised to give you orders. Those orders will be relayed to you via Sergeant Pollard here. I expect instant, unquestioning obedience. I demand that. At least that, and nothing less.'

He paused, looked at the faces of the six listening then continued, 'At this moment, without knowing what might be expected of you, any of you—all of you—may stand up and walk from this room. You'll end up where you began. No criticism. No blame. The last few months will be expunged from your service records.'

Another pause, then, 'As from now, however, you may *not* opt out of the duties you might be asked to perform. Any suggestion that you might *wish* to opt out and you'll be put on ice, held incommunicado and eventually, when *I'm* ready, paraded in front of me to make whatever empty excuses that come to mind.'

A third pause, this time long enough for him to take cigarettes and a lighter from a pocket of his riding breeches, lighting the cigarette, blowing a scarf of smoke and returning the packet and lighter to the pocket.

Then, 'Stand them easy, sergeant.'

'Sah!'

'They may sit down. They may smoke if they wish.'

'Platoon, stand at ease. Stand easy. Take your seats at your respective desks. Smoke if you wish.'

Dansey's smile was cold and without much humour. Nevertheless, it was a smile. This time the impression was that he was taking them into a deep confidence.

'You are the second squad formed for a specific purpose. The first squad—A Squad—was made up of army men. You are all RAF men—and women, of course—you are B Squad. You have each openly expressed a desire to kill enemies of the realm. You have that in common. You have that in common with A Squad.

'For the record, this squad—B Squad—started, like A Squad, with a dozen picked personnel. Two didn't even make it to the start line. Three weren't physically fit enough. One died. Six out of a dozen—a fifty per cent success rate. Not perfect, but we must accept second best when we have no choice.

'You wish to kill enemies of the realm. Not

91

necessarily Germans. But you *will* kill those who oppose this nation, and this nation's war effort. Here in this country, and overseas.

'You will be required to sign the Official Secrets Act. You will most assuredly be required to keep your mouths tightly shut ... otherwise *you* will be looked upon as enemies of the realm.

'You will be taught various ways of killing. All quickly. None too messy. You will become expert in the use of various weapons and equally expert in the use of the weapons nature provided us with. The hands, the arms, the fingers, the feet.

'That is all I need to tell you. But remember what I have told you. In effect, you are an élite squad. Act accordingly. Obey orders without question. Kill when Sergeant Pollard tells you to kill. Do these things, and I rather think you'll enjoy the war.

'One final thing.' He said it as if as an afterthought. 'As from today you all hold commissioned rank. Pilot Officer. The uniforms are already made and waiting to be fitted. The rank is not in order that you may throw your weight around. It is there to prevent the average NCO from throwing *his* weight around.' He dropped what was left of the cigarette and soled it into the stage boarding. Then, 'Thank you, sergeant. That's about all.'

'*Sah!* Platoon, *shun.*'

The quivering salute suggested steel springs, rather than arm muscles. B Squad stood rigid as Dansey left the stage and strode from the hut.

1936

Woodhouse Hill Cemetery was a place of dark greys and dark greens. It was cool and peaceful. It was also uncommonly large. Somewhere, no doubt, there was a tally of the bodies buried within its walls. Certain it is that it was close to being full, and Woodhouse Hill Cemetery, Mk. II had already opened across the road and accepted the overspill of funerals almost eagerly.

The latest burial made its slow progress down the narrow tarmac path. Behind the coffin, the cleric held his Prayer Book open at the appropriate page. If a man of God was allowed to be impatient at a time like this, he was, indeed, impatient. A perfect summer's day. Bird-song galore. And later that afternoon—immediately after this funeral—he was due to exchange his clerical garb for an open-necked shirt, lightweight trousers and an already-packed haversack, and away ... up to the Lake District, holidaying. Mixing with young people, bursting with life and happiness of the Youth Hostel trail and not, as now, suffering the backwash of death and unutterable misery.

Behind the cleric, Chris walked with his mother. Behind them, Seth and Mabel. That was the complete cortège. In life Caleb Calvert had had few friends. In death he had few mourners.

The two women wore black; black coats, black hats with black veils, black shoes and black stockings. Seth wore a suit of charcoal grey tweed, a white shirt and a black tie. Chris wore a navy blue serge suit, also a white shirt and a black tie. Both men looked very uncomfortable in what were obviously newly-bought clothes.

The pitifully small procession made its slow way to the open grave; to the earth-soiled boards at the lip: to the base of the huge sycamore which, with its companion oaks, beeches and elms spread long branches to give Woodhouse Hill Cemetery the gentle shadow which was part of its sombre beauty.

They stood, a silent quartet, while the grave-diggers lowered the coffin; while the cleric intoned the service; while Seth bent to pick up a clod of earth and drop it onto the exposed wood.

Then they left, still in silence, and did not speak until they were beyond the cemetery gates.

The cleric bade them a solemn goodbye, then hurried off for his Lake District holiday.

They stood in a group, on the pavement by the gates; a full two minutes before anybody spoke.

Then Mabel said, 'Why don't you come back with us, Hetty?'

'Oh, no. I've things to do. Things to see to.'

'You'd be welcome. You know that.'

'I know that, but...' Hetty Calvert's voice trailed off into miserable silence.

'Think about it,' urged Mabel. 'There's the spare bedroom. You could stop as long as you like. You wouldn't be a nuisance. Honest.'

Seth growled, 'You're welcome,' but, unlike Mabel, his tone lacked conviction.

Another silence. Awkward and funereal.

Then in a tone made unusually hollow by reason of its false cheerfulness, Mabel said, 'Anyway, Chris will be with you for the next few days. Until you're settled. There's no need to...'

'No!' Chris spoke for the first time. The word was like a tiny explosion. Then, 'I'm going back with you. Not back to Hunslet. Not back *there*.'

'Chris!' Mabel's voice carried shocked outrage.

'I'm not. I don't care what anybody says.'

'Leave it, Mabel.' Hetty's already pale face had blanched to the colour of off-white parchment. She took a deliberate breath, then said, 'I don't blame him. He's a man now. He must make his own decisions.'

95

'For all that,' protested Mabel, 'you can't be left alone. Not at a time like this.'

'I have good neighbours.' A pause, then, 'I'll think on about your offer. I just might come and stay for a few days, when I'm straightened up.'

*　　*　　*

Hetty Calvert had been wrong, of course. Even by the harsh standards of a Hunslet environment, even by the adult decisions he had already had to make as an on-site gamekeeper, Christmas Calvert was *not* a man. A sixteen-year-old youth, 'old for his age' ... not more than that. And the truth was, he didn't fully understand the cold, unfriendly atmosphere on the journey back from Leeds.

'Have I done something wrong?' he'd asked, in the privacy of the compartment of the train.

'Don't *you* think so?' Mabel had glared. 'That was your mother back there. She'd just buried her man ... and you said *that* to her.'

'Her "man"?' he'd muttered bitterly. 'If she's my mother, *he* was my father. But he wasn't, was he? And she isn't. So what does that make me?'

'It makes thee an ungrateful little sod,' Seth had snarled. 'Now, shut thi mouth, or I'll shut it for thi.'

*　　*　　*

96

And that was it. Not another word had been said on the journey, nor when they reached the cottage, nor while Mabel had harnessed Daisy into the shafts of the donkey cart, nor even on the ride out to the van. And the boy's face had remained like rock; as if his facial muscles had set rigid. And Mabel had looked first furiously angry, then unutterably sad, and gradually— very gradually—her mouth had relaxed from the thin-lipped grimness into something more like its long-suffering kindness.

And now she gave a gentle, almost shy smile, and said, 'We've had a bad day, Chris. Both of us.'

'Yes.' It was a short, bitten-off agreement. As if his facial muscles were still cramped and difficult to operate.

She busied them into the van, then returned to the cart to collect a basket of food while he riddled the ash, then filled the kettle and placed it on top of the stove. Queenie scampered out of, then into the van, linking them with tail-wagging, tongue flapping enthusiasm.

Mabel said, 'Shortcake, some apples and a slice of veal and egg pie.'

'Thanks.'

'I'll get one of the under-gardeners to come out tomorrow. There's some more books for you at the cottage.'

'Thanks.'

'Oh, yes. I forgot.' She made it sound like a

sudden recollection. 'The dog—Queenie—she'd better stay with you.'

'Eh?' Chris looked surprised. 'You mean, tonight?'

'Always. She'd better be your dog. Calvert dislikes her. He'll land his boot in her ribs one day. She'll be happier here. A bit of company for you . . . if you want, that is.'

'Yes, please. I want her.' Life came into his eyes and they shone. 'I'd like her. I'd look after her. Honest.'

She smiled at his enthusiasm and said, 'It's what I thought, pet. She'll have a good home. I know that.'

He said, 'Tell Seth.'

'What?'

'She's my dog now. If he tries to kick her again, he'll be sorry. Very sorry.'

'Chris! You mustn't . . .'

'I mean it. Don't think I *don't* mean it. Tell him.'

1942

'A khaki job, name of Montgomery,' said Pollard. 'He's arrived in Egypt with Alexander, and the word is that between them they're going to bloody Rommel's nose.'

Pollard looked as immaculate as ever in his officer-cloth sergeant's uniform; as chunky as

98

ever with his hard-muscled body slightly crouched in front of the easel, on which was pinned a map of North Africa.

He tapped the map with a pointer and continued, 'The Seventh Armoured Division and the Eleven Hussars. They're about "it", until the Eighth Army can be built up into something capable of smashing the Afrika Korps. That means troopships, ammunition ships, supply ships ... the lot. Convoys. *Big* convoys. And for obvious reasons we can't sail through the Med.

'So-o. We go down the west coast of Africa. Up the east coast and through the Suez Canal. But ... and it's a damn big "but" ...

'Rommel's intelligence is good. The convoys take a breather at Freetown. Maybe ship more provisions on board. Maybe unload stuff to be flown in overland. For whatever reason, just about every convoy stops off at Freetown. For starters, it's just about the biggest natural, deep-water harbour in the world. It gives the men in charge of the convoy a break from dodging torpedoes.

'Fine, but a couple of hundred miles north of Freetown is Dakar. Vichy French. A fair-sized oil terminal. A haven for U-boats working the Atlantic. It's there and we can't shift it, and it poses a problem to every convoy sailing in those waters.

'Call in at Freetown, and the chances are that some U-boat will be sniffing around not too far from the harbour mouth, when you leave. The convoys take a hammering. The tankers risk being made into a fireworks display. And they're *there*. Every convoy, as it leaves Sierra Leone.

'Then, south to Lagos. To Nigeria. From there, south to Cape Town and round to Durban. That's a bit far for the average U-boat. A more or less safe journey.' Pollard continued to tap the map with his pointer, as he talked. 'Through the Red Sea. Through the Suez Canal, to Cairo and Alexandria. Then, if this Montgomery character has his way, there's a build-up of troops and equipment until Rommel can be chased out of North Africa.'

Pollard half-turned to face his audience of six pilot officers. He stood with his back to the map, with the pointer held horizontally behind his back. A sardonic grin leered his face as he continued to speak.

'You six have been taught to kill. Right? Straight ways. Fancy ways. Back-to-front ways. Every bloody way there is. And now, you're going to *do* it. Dansey called you the Button Squad. You've been organised for a specific purpose. To make people "disappear". "Vanish". Great ... I'm about to press some buttons.

'Three places. Freetown. Cairo. Alexandria. That's where Rommel's intelligence people are holed up, sending the griff to his front line. He knows the troop movements. He knows what's coming in ... what *hasn't* been sunk by the Dakar U-boats.

'Two of you at each place. Simple orders. Find the bastards then sink *them*.

'Details of each "vanishing trick" in sealed envelopes. You'll open them when you get there. You'll contact who you're told to contact. Three pairs, then. Robertson and D'Souza at Alexandria. Teale and Wisby at Cairo. Calvert and Morton at Freetown. As from now, you're confined to your quarters. No letters. No telephone calls. No nothing. You'll be ready for moving out at five o'clock tomorrow morning.

'I won't wish you luck. If you still need luck, your training's all been a waste of everybody's time.'

* * *

Five hundred years ago, Portuguese navigators landed there, and called it the Mountain of the Lion. Whether from its shape, or whether from the roaring echoes it kicked up in a tropical thunderstorm is not certain. For sure, not because of lions ... there aren't any. Nevertheless, Sierra Leone. At the back end of the sixteenth century Drake dropped in on his voyage round the world. By the 1700s the British were claiming it as part of their expanding empire.

Round about 1787 a group of hyper-do-gooders, cranked up by Wesley's religious fervour, bought a hunk of swamp near the coast from a local chief and shipped more than four hundred freed slaves there, to found a 'Province of Freedom' ... and Freetown came into being.

The place lived up to its names—politely 'The White Man's Grave' or, impolitely 'The Arsehole of the Empire'—the first bunch of freedom-lovers didn't last five years. A second dose was tried in 1792, plus a few hundred Jamaican ex-slaves who were on the run. Thereafter Sierra Leone, and Freetown in particular, became the dropping-off spot for thousands of 'recaptives'—freed slaves from slave ships, intercepted by British navy ships, and merely dumped on the west coast and not, as had been intended, in America.

For a while things went a little out of plumb when the 'recaptives' turned slavers ... but, with one of the biggest natural harbours in the world, the Royal Navy stepped in and returned things to a more or less acceptable level.

Nevertheless and with that brand of history to fall back on, Sierra Leone in general, and Freetown in particular, remained one of the main contestants for the title of smelliest, most disease-ridden and disgustingly filthy places on God's earth.

This, in 1942.

Pilot Officers Christmas Calvert and Avril

Morton knew little of the history, but much of the truth as they sat with the man from the Elder Dempster depot, in a corner of the open-fronted, Syrian bar in Kissy Street. All three were in lightweight khaki. The faces of all three were shiny with perspiration while, outside, the rain came down with a fury the two-foot-deep channels on each side of the road could hardly cope with.

'Rainy season,' grunted the Elder Dempster man. 'It's just about getting into its stride.'

Chris said, 'The sooner we're back with civilised weather the better.'

The E. D. man grinned. He was a typical 'colonial' type; bleach-haired, tobacco-roughed voiced, tanned-skinned, and peering, half-closed eyes. He added, 'The boys are used to it, of course.'

'The boys?' Chris asked the question.

'The blacks, Timne and Mende, mainly. But there's a fair splash of Krios around. And of course Syrians ... like the joker who runs this bar.'

'You live here?' Avril's question was shot with near disbelief.

'Twenty years.' The grin reappeared. 'I wanted to come back—join some mob—when the war came. But London insisted I stay here, and keep an eye on things.'

'Like who's on our side, and who isn't?' suggested Chris.

'Something like that.'

103

'And?'

'Y'see, Calvert.' The E.D. man leaned over the table a little. 'Forget the "king and country" guff. *This* is their country. The only one they know. And what little good there is here, *we're* creaming off. Their allegiance—whatever allegiance they have—is to their own tribal chiefs. The wise men of the village. Show them a map. They don't know where London is.'

'And Berlin?' asked Chris.

'Or Berlin,' said the E.D. man. 'They know what money is. They know what being scared is.' He finished his whisky, then went on, 'Secret societies, old man. That's what scares the hell out of 'em. Most of the men are in the Poro society ... and various branches. Most of the women in the Bundu society. The Bundu is *very* "closed shop". Fertility rites. Arsing around with virginity. That sort of thing. But the boys ... they just play at make-believe voodoo.'

'Make-believe?' It was Avril who asked the question.

'*They* believe.' The grin came again. 'Leopard society stuff. Crap, done up in painted faces and animal skins. Black magic, if you like. At a guess, they make it up as they go along.'

'They frighten each other?' suggested Chris.

'It doesn't take much doing. When they're born, they're half-way to believing.'

'They scare easily and they take bribes,' mused Chris.

'I know.' The E.D. man nodded. 'The Germans pay them well, and scare the hell out of them.'

'So-o. We pay them more and scare them worse.'

'It's a game.'

'We have to win.'

'Yeah.' The E.D. man sucked in his breath, then said, 'There's one way. It means taking chances, but I know some of the boys from the West African Frontier Force. They'll do anything—*anything*—to crap on the locals. If you're prepared to take a chance...'

Chris said, 'It's why we're here.'

'Okay. The rain should stop for a spell within the next day or two. The harmattan wind will dry things out in less than twenty-four hours. Then—if we're ready—we should be able to make them crap thunderbolts.'

* * *

Chris marvelled that such a hell-hole could be so beautiful. King Tom Cemetery stank of rotting vegetation and worse, but the waist-high elephant grass glittered and danced with fireflies enough to give the impression of a miniaturised torchlight rally. Countless frogs croaked their unmusical noise into the night, but overhead a black, velvet sky showed a

105

shower of diamonds and a moon as bright as a silver sickle.

He'd been there, standing behind the bole of a tree, for all of three hours. He'd seen the khaki figures of the West African Frontier Force men herd the natives from the burying ground and, hopefully, they were now in position for the next phase of the night's work.

The E.D. man had been very sure. He had the 'connections'. He knew what to say, and who to tell it to. But as far as Chris was concerned, this was unknown territory. Already he hated Africa. Africa in general, and this place in particular.

The E.D. man had said, 'Mind where you go, Chris. They don't always fill the graves up in a hurry, and they don't go in for fripperies like coffins.'

'Christ!'

'Very basic, old son. This is Africa, not Highgate.'

Way out in the distance—and gone to hell beyond the sea's horizon—reflected flashes of the continuous electrical storms rippled the darkness slightly. Too far away to hear any thunder. Too far away for it to make any real difference to the blackness. In the old days the moors had been lonely, but this was a different and, in some way, a more intense, more hemmed in loneliness. A distilled loneliness. A suffocating loneliness.

The E.D. man had warned, 'You won't see

them, old man. You'll see Avril before you see *them*, but they'll be there. Bet on it.'

Away to the left a vague smudge of lightness marked the King Tom Naval Base. But the matelots rarely sought the dingy fleshpots of Freetown and the officers would be sniffing around the nursing sisters at the Fifty-First Hospital, a good five miles inland.

The E.D. man had said, 'The main path, through the cemetery. That's the way they'll come. And using Avril as bait, we can't go wrong.'

Chris felt the comforting weight of the Savage repeating rifle on his forearm; 30/30 calibre, lever action, one shot in the breech and five others waiting in the magazine. A gun like that could end most arguments satisfactorily ... if only there was something to aim at.

Quite suddenly, he saw Avril strolling down the path towards him. Literally *strolling*! He also saw the grotesque figure prancing quietly in her wake. A native with a massive representation of an erect phallus strapped to his groin. Body naked, except for this monstrous outrage. But with a leopard skull on his head and the hide hanging down his back, with the skin of the forelegs draped across his shoulders. He danced silently in her wake and, as he danced, he waved a short-handled, short-thonged whip in each hand. Each whip had four thongs, and woven in each thong was a pair of large fish-hooks.

Chris dropped the Savage from the crook of his arm to a waiting hand and, as he did so, the strangling cord flipped round his neck and was jerked tight.

He let the Savage fall to the ground and reached upward to take the constriction from his throat, but his fingers couldn't find enough leverage to get beneath the cord. He felt his eyes bulging and the blood start to pump at his temples.

He saw the thing behind Avril deliberately attract her attention. Saw her turn, then dip her hand into the shoulder bag she was carrying. He heard the single shot and saw the leopard man crumple and fall.

For a moment he almost blacked out, as the strangling cord suddenly tightened even more. Then, there was a gurgling gasp, the cord slackened and a weight fell against his back.

He ripped the cord free, turned and saw the E.D. man drawing the blood-soaked sword-stick from the black's ribs.

'Start shooting,' snapped the E.D. man.

Chris stooped, grabbed the Savage and followed the advice.

It was, as he later admitted, something of a turkey shoot. This was especially so when, after the first couple of shots, the Frontier Force men fired the petrol-soaked elephant grass on the perimeter of the cemetery. The natives dashed for the path, were silhouetted against the flames and dropped as the rifle was pointed and the trigger squeezed. In truth he didn't shoot to kill and, other than the leopard man, nobody *was* killed. But blood was spilled and bones were shattered and, in less than five minutes—less than two re-loads of the magazine—the few natives left were haring for some sort of safety and away from the centre of this disgusting place of general death.

*   *   *

More than fifty miles inland from Freetown, in the village of Magburaka, Chris and the E.D. man sat at the entrance to the chief's thatched hut. The place was away from the swamps of the shore, but the 'bush'—the green-heavy jungle—hemmed the village in and gave a feeling of suffocating claustrophobia.

They'd come in by truck, accompanied by half a dozen Frontier Force men and, on the way, the E.D. man had again passed local knowledge and wisdom to Chris.

'Morgan—God only knows why "Morgan", but that's his name—Tombo Morgan. The local chief, and the hound who's in the pay of the Dakar crowd. Oh, he'll deny it, and the guy who organised things at the coast will be there to save the chief's face, but *he's* the one you'll be paying, when the general shakes have died down.'

'He knows we're coming?' Chris's question was shot with surprise.

109

'There's not a lot these village bosses don't know.'

'In that case...'

'Old son, don't ask too many questions. There aren't enough answers. My information is that the transmitter was somewhere on top of the hill, by Fourah Bay College. It's more than likely, but we'd never have found it. This is the best way. Scare the buggers, then bribe them.'

And now they were sitting on old-fashioned kitchen chairs outside the chief's hut, with the chief sitting between them on a high-backed, swivel, executive's chair ... his 'throne'.

The chief was saying, 'You come making complaint. Yes?'

'Yes.' The E.D. man nodded. 'We come making bad complaint.'

'Him boss?' The chief nodded towards Chris.

'Him big boss,' said the E.D. man. 'Him big boss from king chief boss, England.'

'King chief boss complains?'

'Too bloody true, boy. King chief boss not at all pleased.'

'With Tombo Morgan?' The chief put on a look of shocked surprise.

'Very much with Tombo Morgan.'

'Ah!'

'King chief boss figure maybe Tombo Morgan slapped on big ship. Maybe taken back to England. Maybe even given big chop.'

110

Morgan looked as if he'd suddenly been slapped across the face. Nor was it play-acting.

The E.D. man said, 'Maybe boss Calvert help. Maybe him even *believe* Tombo Morgan.'

Chris dutifully scowled.

Morgan growled, 'Tombo Morgan not know things. How Tombo Morgan understand if he not know things?'

'Tombo Morgan's boy,' said the E.D. man. 'Him send message to king chief boss's enemies about big ships in harbour.'

'Why for should Tombo Morgan do these things?'

'King chief's enemies dash Tombo Morgan's boy plenty. That's why.'

'No dash Tombo Morgan.'

'No?'

'No dash Tombo Morgan,' repeated Morgan. 'Tombo Morgan's boy do something Tombo Morgan not know?' The E.D. man put almost unbelievable surprise into the question.

'Tombo Morgan know,' grated Morgan. 'Tombo Morgan *always* know about his boys.'

'Leopard boys?' Again the tone of the question suggested that the E.D. man was surprised.

'Tombo Morgan know. Nobody tell Tombo Morgan *anything*.'

'Right!' Suddenly there was a whiplash quality in the E.D. man's voice. It brought the group of thirty or so villagers standing in a half-circle in front of their chief a fraction nearer. A fraction more menacing. It made the half-dozen Frontier Force men suddenly straighten to attention and touch the grips of their sheathed machetes. It warned Chris that whatever politenesses that had been necessary were over. Hard talk was about to begin.

The E.D. man snapped, 'The easy way, or the bloody hard way. That's something Tombo Morgan had better understand. Those Leopard Society buggers Tombo Morgan knows all about tried to kill boss Calvert's woman three nights ago. They slashed her arm and ripped her shirt. That, I take it, is something else Tombo Morgan knows all about.'

'Tombo Morgan know,' muttered Morgan.

'Tombo Morgan had better pull himself together, then. Right? Else king chief boss might wage war on Tombo Morgan.'

'Tombo Morgan not wage war on king chief boss.'

'It should be a bloody walk-over, then. Shouldn't it?'

'Tombo Morgan sorry,' mumbled Morgan. 'You tell king chief boss, Tombo Morgan sorry.'

There was a silence. Tombo Morgan had a worried frown on his face. The E.D. man stayed expressionless and tapped his malacca cane on the hard earth. It seemed to mean nothing, but it was a signal.

112

Chris snapped, 'Manaboy Kamara.'

'What?' Tombo Morgan jerked his head, as if from a slap in the face.

'Manaboy Kamara.'

'What you know...'

'Manaboy Kamara,' barked Chris for the third time.

'Who the hell's Manaboy Kamara?' asked the E.D. man, and looked almost forlorn with an expression of pained puzzlement.

Morgan muttered, 'Kamara Tombo Morgan's nephew. Tombo Morgan's mother's sister's son. Tombo Morgan not know about Kamara.'

'*What* about Kamara?'

Reluctantly, Morgan said, 'Kamara do wrong things.'

'*What* wrong things?'

'Kamara friend of king chief boss's enemies.'

'Tombo Morgan know *everything*,' the E.D. man reminded him.

'Not know about Kamara till today.'

'Ah!' The E.D. man waited.

Morgan looked a little sheepish, tried a tentative grin, got no response then instead scowled and clapped his hands imperiously.

He said, 'Tombo Morgan bring Kamara here. No waste time. Tombo Morgan friend of king chief boss.'

The half-circle of villagers parted and two men dragged a reluctant third to a spot slightly

113

less than a yard in front of the village chief's chair.

'Manaboy Kamara,' said Morgan triumphantly. 'He make leopard boy trouble. He take dash from king chief boss's enemies. Now Tombo Morgan punish Manaboy Kamara.'

The E.D. man said, 'Tombo Morgan could be in big trouble.'

'No!' Morgan raised his hands in make-believe horror. 'Tombo Morgan do nothing. *Nothing*. Manaboy Kamara do wrong things. Now Tombo Morgan punish Manaboy Kamara. You see. You be happy. King chief boss be happy. Boss Calvert be happy.'

The E.D. man growled, 'Keep your fingers crossed, boy. You just might *not* be held responsible.'

*   *   *

The Ford truck rattled its way back to Freetown. Along pot-holed roads, already dusty despite the recent downpour. Across shallow, broad-flowing streams where, it was rumoured, diamonds could be found if panned for. On both sides the bush closed in like a mottled green, candlewick curtain. The stench from nearby swamp-land permeated everywhere.

Chris and the E.D. man shared the cab with the Frontier Force driver.

114

Chris asked, 'Will he?'

'What?'

'Behave himself? Stop feeding information to Dakar?'

'He'll stop,' said the E.D. man confidently. Then, 'Some other greedy smart-arse will take his place ... eventually. But give it a couple of months.'

'A complete waste of time,' grunted Chris.

'We'll know who, within a week.'

'In that case, why...'

'Let it happen, then stamp on it. That's the best way.'

'Oh!'

They bumped and growled along for another ten minutes or so before the E.D. man spoke again.

He said, 'Avril handled the Leopard Society business very well.'

'You told us to expect it.'

'Nevertheless.' He shrugged his shoulders. 'It can be a mite off-putting, in the middle of a cemetery.'

'Why did they do it?'

'To give you the quakes. See how easily you scare.'

'And?'

'You're Morgan's juju man now.'

'Eh?'

'Manaboy Kamara. Less than a week here, and you knew all about him ... and *he's* Morgan's boy.'

'But you told. The name didn't mean a damn thing to *me*.'

'Morgan didn't know that. As far as he's concerned you came ashore, worked some sort of high class juju, and knew one of his most closely guarded secrets.'

'A cheap conjuring trick,' said Chris.

'It doesn't matter if we use mirrors,' grunted the E.D. man. 'If we get what we want, everybody's happy.'

'And Manaboy Kamara?' asked Chris.

'Morgan will handle him.'

'How?'

'At a guess, stake him out over an ant-hill for twenty-four hours.'

'Christ!'

'A few hundred thousand of those little buggers nipping you all day. It tends to change the outlook a little.'

'It'll kill him? Is that what you mean?'

'Not kill him. Send him crazy, perhaps. That's what happens sometimes. They cut him loose and he can't think straight. He wanders off into the bush. He's rarely seen again.'

Again Chris breathed, 'Christ!'

Deliberately—laconically—the E.D. man said, 'It tends to dampen down any over-enthusiasm.'

*   *   *

Chris and the E.D. man had had a good night's

sleep. They'd showered, shaved and breakfasted. It was still mid-morning, but the Royal Navy corvette, anchored out in the harbour, seemed anxious to weigh anchor and get under way. The two men stood on the quay, near the steps leading down to the waiting launch. They were alone and standing apart from the normal build-up of activity on the quay. Avril was already aboard the corvette, hopefully having the slash from the fish hook treated.

The E.D. man was saying, 'Those wounds. Nothing in normal circumstances, but out here I've known razor nicks turn septic.'

'They'll see to her.'

There was an awkwardness, as if they were reluctant to leave each other.

The E.D. man said, 'Give my regards to the first oak you come across.'

'I'll do that.'

'And Claude. Give him my regards.'

'Who?'

'Dansey. Claude Dansey. The man who sent you out here.'

'I—er—I didn't realise you were...'

'It's a tight circle, old cock. We met in America. He tends to use everybody he ever meets ... eventually.'

'Oh! I see.'

'Give him my love.' A quick smile, then, 'In less than a week you'll be seeing Liverpool waterfront. I envy you, Chris.'

'If the U-boats don't get us.'

'A small naval vessel? A corvette? Economics, my son. It's not worth the cost of a torpedo.'

Chris hefted his service haversack into a more comfortable position, then held out his hand.

'It's been good meeting you.'

'Me, too.' They shook hands, then the E.D. man held out the malacca cane. 'Take it. You should find more use for it. As a reminder of West Africa ... if only that.'

'Thanks.'

Chris took the sword-stick, then, rather gingerly, descended the steps to the waiting launch.

1936

It was a cold, hard winter up on the tops. The van's slow combustion stove was never allowed to burn itself out and, every ten days or so, Mabel brought out two sacks of coke in the donkey cart.

In late November she brought out a wireless set; fret-fronted and with a dry battery and an accumulator. She showed him how to string an aerial along one inside wall of the van; how to link up the earth wire to a steel bar driven into the ground outside the van. How to operate

118

and tune the set.

'And keep an eye on the batteries, pet. I'll change the accumulator every fortnight or so. Charlie, the chauffeur, has re-charging equipment in his garage.'

And yet, Chris used the wireless set very little. He preferred his books, and his trudges through the snow with Queenie at his heels. He learned to read the snow-prints. The single, 'tightrope' marks left by a fox; so different from a dog's footprints. The run and feathery wing-spread of a pheasant taking off from the covering of whiteness. The snake-like run of the weasel and the stoat. The 'exclamation marks' of the rabbit. The faint, ragged strokes of field mice and voles.

And yet, he listened to the 'woman-I-love' speech broadcast by the monarch who was not yet a complete monarch and, like so many of the subjects of this king, he was shocked and outraged.

'Why?' he demanded of the tail-wagging dog. And the dog listened obediently. 'Why is he such a ninny? Doesn't he *know*? He's not ordinary. He's royal. Regal. He's not *allowed* to put some calf-eyed woman before his duty to the rest of us.'

Then he switched off the wireless set and opened the book he was reading, and forgot himself in a world of magnificent make-believe.

*　　*　　*

The snow quietened, but the frost hardened. Hedges and dry-stone walls were garlanded with silver-thickened spiders' webs, and every overhang had its own necklace of icicles. It was a cold world, but a fine world, and the Smiths had hauled their caravan into the lee of the cliff alongside Blackwater Tarn.

Chris was glad to see them and, as a greeting gift, carried two recently shot rabbits for their pot. The tarn was frozen over and two of the Smiths' offspring were using the surface as a slide; racing towards the frozen water, across the slight slope of shingle, then skidding, stiff-legged over the smooth ice.

It can be said that both Chris and Jared Smith saw the danger at the same time. They both yelled a warning, and they were both too late. The ice cracked with an almost lazy deliberation and the boy farthest from the shore shrieked, flung his arms into the air then disappeared into the water alongside the frozen surface.

Chris dropped the rabbits and his gun and raced along the shore line.

He shouted, 'Get a rope.'

Jared stopped his own dash for the ice, turned and grabbed a coil from a hook near the van's axle.

They met, Chris snatched one end of the rope, gasped, 'Hang on,' then, as he ran

120

towards the broken ice, fastened the rope around his middle. He threw himself forward for the last few yards, skidded spread-eagled on the surface towards the break, saw the boy's arms and terrified face above the water, stretched and encircled the boy's middle with his arms then, as the ice broke further, went into the water of the tarn with the boy.

The cold of the water was like a vice across his chest. He was unable to breathe. He couldn't swim and for a split second he almost allowed panic to take over. Then he forced himself to remain calmer, tightened his grip on the boy and fought unconsciousness until the sheer pain, combined with the cold and the inability to breathe, forced insensibility onto him.

He regained consciousness in the Smiths' van. He was naked in front of the stove and Morven Smith was rubbing circulation into his body with a rough textured hard cloth. He was slumped in a chair and as he came to Morven said, 'You're worse than the boy, lad. We thought you were dead.'

'I'm all right.' The scrubbing of the rough material was like blunted nails scoring into his skin, but feeling was coming back fast. He asked, 'How is the boy?'

'Cold, but not as cold as you.' She stood back and said, 'Up onto the bed, lad, and let me rub real life back into you.'

Obediently, he climbed a little unsteadily

into the bunk bed and flopped face down on a surprisingly soft mattress. He gave tiny grunts of pleasure as she kneaded warm life into his shoulders and back; pummelled his muscles and worked new blood to the surface. As she massaged, she talked.

'The two boys are scared. Serves them right. They're tucked up warm in the tent. Maybe Jared will let them get dressed and play around when he gets back. I doubt it. You feeling better now, lad?'

'Much better, thanks.'

'Right, turn over onto your back.'

Chris did as he was told and she started at the shoulders again, then worked down the arms. The chest, the ribs, the stomach muscles. And all the while she talked in short-sentenced bursts of conversation.

'Jared's gone to the hall. To tell your aunt. He's grateful. We're both grateful. He won't be long.' Then she was at the crotch; working the muscles on his inner thighs. Quite suddenly she grasped him, firmly but gently, and smiled down into his startled face. 'You're a man now, lad. More of a man than I expected. Mark what I say. One day you'll send some woman crazy. You're lucky, Chris. *She'll* be lucky, too.'

Thirty minutes later he was huddled in ancient army blankets, in the donkey cart, on his way to the gamekeeper's cottage.

Mabel said, 'You could have been drowned.'

'I wasn't.'

122

'You saved the little one's life. You know that?'

'Maybe.'

'The gypsy knows it. *He's* grateful. His wife too, I expect.'

'Oh, yes. *She's* grateful.' His lips twitched upwards in the ghost of a smile.

'All we need now is to get you into some dry clothes and into a warm bed. You should come to no harm.'

*   *   *

At mid-morning next day Smith visited the gamekeeper's van. He rode the skewbald mare which hauled the caravan and he carried a large pie, wrapped in a brightly coloured kerchief.

He knocked at the van door and, when Chris invited him inside, he unknotted the kerchief and placed the pie dish on top of the slow combustion stove.

'Rabbit pie,' he announced. 'With root vegetable and some herbs. Morven said to tell you it will give you strength.'

'Thanks.' Chris motioned to a chair. 'Stay. Share it with me.'

'No. I thank you, but no. I have things to do.' There was a silence. Awkward. Then, hesitantly, Smith said, 'I owe you, Christmas Calvert. I owe you a life.'

'Don't be silly. Anybody would have...'

123

'No. They wouldn't. Not "anybody". You've become a friend, and I'm deeply in your debt.'

'I—er—I'm pleased. Of course we're friends.'

'If you want me. Any time. For anything. If I'm not around these parts, ask at Appleby. The Horse Fair. They'll know. Somebody will know. They'll tell me.'

'Thanks, but—y'know—I'll bear that in mind. If ever I want a favour, that is.'

1942

'Orders from Dansey,' said Pollard. 'A personal request from Churchill. Things can't come from a higher shelf than that.'

Chris nodded and wondered what was on its way.

They'd been met on the dock side by a brace of service policemen. One had guided Avril to Lime Street and the next train north. The other had taken Chris to St Anne Street Police Station, there to meet Pollard who'd taken over, bustled Chris into a staff car, climbed behind the wheel and driven south, out of the city. And now, as the bomb-blasted buildings and the bird-topped Liver building disappeared through the rear window, Pollard talked.

124

He said, 'Remember your Oath of Allegiance? You took it when you joined.'

'Of course.'

'And the affirmation you signed, when you started in with Dansey's people?'

'Of course. Why do you ask?'

'Just making sure you know where you stand. This job isn't firing some shots at a bunch of nig-nogs. Upset *this* little apple cart, and you could end up facing a treason charge.'

'Christ!'

'Just bear that in mind, and listen.' Pollard settled back to drive along a moderately straight stretch of road. Thereafter his voice had a sing-song quality; as if he'd memorised notes and knew exactly what he was going to say, long before he said it.

'B Squad. Remember? The Button Squad. Press the right button and somebody is "vanished". I rather like that. Very descriptive. Very impressive. And you at this moment are very much the right button. Somebody—a very important "somebody"—must be "vanished" ... and yet *not* "vanished".'

They halted at traffic lights and Pollard remained silent until the lights turned to green then, as he flicked the lever up the gears, he continued.

'The visitor who dropped in last May. The unexpected visitor. The *unwanted* visitor. Rudolph Hess. Hitler's deputy, no less, dropping in by parachute and landing in the wilds of Scotland.

'You have no idea of the fluttering in the dovecotes. He claimed to be on a peace mission. To stop the war. As if the crazy bastard *could*. But that's what he claimed. What he still claims ... and Calvert, you have no idea of the shit that's been pumped into him to make him change his tune. To make him tell what the real truth is.'

'And?' asked Chris.

'Sure, he wanted peace.' The tone was ugly with contempt. 'His beloved bloody Germany. Hitler was going for Russia ... less than a month after Hess landed. The old German cock-up. War on two fronts. They never learn. Hess thought he could pull the chestnuts out of the fire. Peace in Europe, while they knocked blue hell out of Russia. *Then* finish Europe off.'

'You think?'

'I *know*. The boys with the hypodermics have milked the sod dry. Deputy to the big man himself? He *had* to be given mink-lined treatment.' Pollard chuckled quietly. The sound was much like a death-rattle. He went on, 'But Churchill wouldn't even *see* him. He wanted him out. Kaput. Finis.

'A lot of miscalculations, y'see. They didn't realise how much Winnie hates the Ruskies. Never trusted Honest Joe Stalin. Let the German Army cripple the Red Army ... then *we* go in and mop up what's left. It's called "strategy". That's how Churchill calculates the long-term end.

'And, within limits, he's right. From what Hess has said, even Hitler has doubts about Britain *and* Russia. Strange, that.' Again the death-rattle chuckle. 'Britain, Germany and Russia. Nobody seems to give a piss-in-the-wind damn about the Italians ... or the Yanks. It's *our* war. The rest are just corner-men.'

*　　*　　*

Four hours later, Chris was lost. With the wartime absence of signposts and place names, only the position of the sun in the heavens had given him a clue as to their direction of travel. South—he knew south. And west—occasionally they seemed to be driving directly into the late afternoon sun.

They hadn't stopped for meals. They hadn't even broken the journey for petrol. Just on and on at a steady, distance-consuming speed, skirting built-up areas—Chris had realised this—until they were gradually surrounded by a wildness as bleak, and bleaker, than that Chris had keepered over. Rising and falling hills; great distances of weather-torn moorland, criss-crossed sparsely by little more than dirt tracks.

Pollard growled, 'Brecon Beacons. Wilder than Dartmoor, I reckon. The War Office use it for toughening up the troops.'

'Wales?' queried Chris.

127

'Yeah. Taffy-Land. We'll be there in no time at all.'

'Where?'

'Where we're going. Where we'll eat and drink. And sleep. Where you'll do what we came out to do.'

Five more miles or thereabouts, a branch off to the right, an incline to the top of a knoll, followed by a steep descent, then round the shoulder of a steep, hump-backed hill, and there it was. As honest a piece of Victorian stonework as could be found in the whole of the United Kingdom. Rising almost straight out of the turf; mullioned windows, pillars at the entrance, a small forest of chimneys and the encouragement of an immediate and obvious question, which Chris asked.

'What the hell is it? And how the hell did it get *here*?'

'It's a "folly", son.' Pollard halted the car at the main entrance. 'This prat had more cash than sense. He wanted solitude, but he also demanded comfort. Lots of both. Unmarried. No relations. When he snuffed it the Government took over.' The nasty chuckle came again. 'Safer than most prisons. People *not* escaping get lost and die on Brecon Beacons. Regularly.' As they left the car and walked to the house, he continued, 'we use it almost all the time these days. De-briefing. Deep interviewing. Making people think they're guests when, in fact, they're prisoners.

It's very useful ... and practically unknown.'

* * *

Four of them sat at the table. Chris, Pollard, Hess and the translator. They ate, and what they ate was both civilised and expertly served; chicken soup that had never seen a tin, Welsh lamb chops with new potatoes, baby carrots, broccoli and mint sauce, apple pie and cream. Then real coffee, biscuits and cheese. There was a war on, food rationing was making people tighten their belts a new notch every month or so, but here, in this hideaway in the Brecon Beacons, the food was good and sufficient.

Part-way through the soup, Hess had growled some bad-tempered remark.

The translator—a middle-aged civilian, podgy, balding and wearing thick-rimmed spectacles—had smiled apologetically and said, 'Herr Hess says he intends to make a formal complaint. He considers it an insult that he should share his table with NCOs and junior officers.'

Chris looked at Pollard questioningly.

Pollard scooped up another spoonful of soup, then lowered the spoon, dabbed his lips with his napkin and very deliberately said, 'Please tell Herr Hess that he can kiss my arse.'

The translator's lips quivered in an embarrassed half-smile.

Pollard said, 'Go on. Tell him.'

The translator spoke in German. Hess's shoulders moved in a tiny shrug. His expression suggested that he had suddenly become aware of a nasty smell. He continued with his soup.

Nothing more was said throughout the meal.

*　　*　　*

Chris was awakened next morning at five-thirty. A corporal batman shook him gently by the shoulder and motioned to a mug of steaming hot tea on the bedside table.

'Message from Sergeant Pollard, sir. Drink that. It's laced with rum. Then will you please report to him, in the hall, at six hundred hours. Clean, shaved and in best blue.'

A quick shower in the en suite bathroom, followed by a shave, then the donning of a newly pressed uniform, and he was walking into the hall as the hands of the wall clock showed 6 a.m. exactly.

'End of Hess.' Pollard wasted no time on polite preliminaries. He turned towards the door. 'A turn outside to breathe good Welsh air, before we go downstairs.'

'Downstairs?' Chris fell in step and they descended the shallow steps to the gravel surround of the house.

'The cellars. Dungeons, really. That's where

he is. Has been for weeks.'

'Except for meals.' Chris made it a near-question.

'Eh? Oh!' Pollard smiled. He said, 'That? Last night?' They strolled about ten steps in silence, then Pollard continued, 'I think you should know. After that, no more speculation, but a tightly closed mouth.' He said, 'That wasn't Hess, last night. Not the *real* Hess.'

'Oh!'

'Doubles, Calvert. The Psychological War outfit play at "Doubles". Churchill has one. Maybe more than one. Alexander has one. This Montgomery lad will have one, if he becomes important enough. Well known. Rommel has at least one. At a guess, Hitler and his whole gang have one each. It's necessary, these days. It keeps the opposition guessing. Does the dirty on would-be assassins.'

They turned the corner and crunched up the side of the folly. Pollard talked. Chris listened.

'God knows why the clown dropped in in the first place. The boffins have milked him dry. Truth drugs ... and more. The trouble is, he's completely screwed up by this time. Completely nuts, and if the International Red Cross—Sweden, Spain, Switzerland—get even a whiff, *they'll* go nuts.'

'So you've replaced the real one with a double?' Chris figured it was time he said something.

'It wasn't too difficult.' Pollard's mouth

131

twisted into his own version of a smile. 'The Isle of Man. Thousands of German nationals, rounded up when the war started. Plus what PoWs we've got our hands on in the North African campaign. It wasn't *too* difficult. The dental records differ, of course, and there's a small scar. And the fingerprints, of course. But nobody's likely to look too closely. Hess arrived here. Hess is locked up, pending a decision about what to do with him. It's not too involved, really.'

'But the *real* Hess?' Chris wanted to be sure he'd got things right.

'Oh, we bury *him*.' Pollard made it a slight, lightweight remark. 'Out on the Beacons, somewhere. As good a resting place as any. A damn sight too good for that bastard.'

*   *   *

Indeed, it was a dungeon, rather than a cellar. Complete with vaulted roof and tiny, high, securely barred window. A metal chair was bolted to the stone flags of the room. A metal bed, covered with a palliasse-like mattress and two army blankets. And that was it. Nothing else. An average police cell was luxurious by comparison.

Hess—the *real* Hess—was sitting on the chair. He was wearing a white, cotton-type boiler suit and sandals. He was staring into nowhere, and the beetling brows looked like a cliff overhang above the sunken eyes. His hair had been cut short, and he wore a two-day growth of beard. He looked bad. Empty and not aware of what was going on around him.

On the way to the dungeon, Pollard had collected a holstered pistol from a safe near the head of the stairs. As they entered the dungeon he slipped the weapon from its holster and handed it to Chris.

'Don't waste too much time. Get the film running, then do the job.'

'Film?' Chris blinked.

'The Powers-that-Be. Churchill in particular. They want proof. As near as dammit to being here. No mistakes. No kidology.'

'That's sick,' complained Chris.

'If they want to be sick, kinky ... anything. They have the clout, Calvert. If they want it set to music, that's how we deliver.'

Pollard reached for a spot just above the jamb of the cell door. There was the gentle sound of quiet, well-oiled machinery running and, from a top corner of the cell, the single eye of a camera stared down at them.

Hess seemed quite unaware of his visitors, or the new sound.

Pollard said, 'The nape of the neck. Then when he's on the floor, a couple into his head for good measure.'

'Is that quite necessary?' murmured Chris.

'It's necessary. Otherwise, I wouldn't

133

have said.'

Chris obeyed orders. He stepped to the chair, put the muzzle of the pistol to within an inch of the nape of Hess's neck, then squeezed the trigger. In the confined space the explosion of the round was unnaturally loud. Hess fell forward and sprawled on the stone floor. He was very obviously dead; the exiting round had carried half his face away and blood was everywhere.

'And the rest,' growled Pollard.

Chris stepped round the chair, tilted the pistol and sent two more rounds into the head.

As they left the cell Pollard said, 'Up north now. You'll stop for breakfast on the way. You'll be back at Goy Castle before nightfall.'

Chris grunted a non-reply and handed the pistol back to Pollard.

1937

High Wind Bank looked beautiful in its stark emptiness, and the top of Old Cote Moor showed low-lying smoke, rolling towards Kilnsey, where the Skirfare joined the Wharfe.

Christmas Calvert stood on a rise and watched the scene across a long, low valley. The man standing alongside him lowered field-glasses, and spoke.

'Will it reach here?'

'No.' Chris sounded quite sure. 'The heather and bracken are dry. Dead. They'll burn. Smoulder, at least. From the top, it's turf. That won't burn.'

The man glanced at him and said, 'You sound very sure.'

'The turf won't burn,' repeated Chris. 'Our game is quite safe.'

The man, Sir Arnold Baxter, allowed a quick smile to touch his lips. He gave the impression of a man who smiled easily; thin-lipped, but wide-mouthed. He was a slim man, without being thin. His facial skin was weather-beaten and well lined. He wore a deerstalker, a turtle-necked sweater, an open-necked, lumberjack shirt, a belted Norfolk jacket, flannel slacks and brogues.

He said, 'I meant to ask you. You've never taken a holiday since you came here. Any real reason?' Then, hurriedly, 'Not that I'm prying. It's none of my business, really.'

'This is holiday enough,' said Chris.

'Ah.' The quick smile came and went.

Chris said, 'People pay good money to walk in this sort of scenery. I get paid for doing it. I don't need a holiday.'

'You sound a very contented young man.'

'I am.'

There was a silence, for all of a minute. The dog, Queenie, sat motionless by Chris's heel and both men watched the smoke roll across the moorland.

Quite suddenly Baxter said, 'I'm thinking of doing without your uncle.'

It was quietly spoken, and Chris made no reaction.

Baxter went on, 'I don't have to tell you. He's fond of his drink. Probably too fond. He's becoming even more unpopular with the other estate workers and I hear rumours that his private life isn't all it should be.'

'He likes men,' said Chris bluntly.

'Ah.'

'Rather than women, I mean.'

'Quite.' Then, gently, 'Not with you, I hope.'

'Not with me.'

'Forgive me for asking . . . but it's illegal, you know.'

'I know.'

Again there was a silence. They watched the smoke, with a thin line of orange at its base.

Baxter said, 'Would you like his job? Head keeper, I mean.'

'There's a couple of others, older than me.'

'I know. But they're in the Territorial Army. They may not be here for long.'

Chris turned his head and asked, 'Is there going to be a war?'

'Some of my friends who've visited Germany think so. The Nazi party mean business and this Hitler fellow seems set on it.'

Chris said, 'I can't take the job. Thanks, but I can't. It would mean Aunt Mabel losing her home.'

136

'Not Mabel.' The smile did its quick appearance. 'He loses his job, but I won't put Mabel on the street.'

Chris took a deep breath, then said, 'Why not make *her* head keeper?'

'Eh?' Baxter raised surprised eyebrows.

'She knows as much about game rearing as he does. And she's a fine shot.'

'It wouldn't do.' Then there was a hesitant pause and, 'No. It wouldn't do. The other two might not like it that way.'

* * *

Queenie awakened him. He'd been asleep perhaps an hour. No more. It had been late dusk when he'd climbed into the bed, and it wasn't yet dark enough to completely black out the window of the van. The dog growled from deep in its throat.

'Quiet, Queenie.'

From outside came the shouts of drunken rage.

'You ungrateful young bugger. Come on! Come out here, and I'll blow you to hell and back.'

Then came the roar of a twelve-bore and the pellets rattled into the side of the van.

'Come on. Let's be seeing you. You miserable little bastard.'

Chris swung his legs from the bed and reached for the Savage. He motioned for the dog to stay where it was. He unbolted the door of the van, pushed it open a little, then had it slammed shut, as more shotgun pellets smashed into the woodwork.

He bent his knee into his stomach, put the flat of his foot onto the woodwork of the door, and straightened his leg. The door flew open, he tumbled outside, rolled on the turf and finished on his belly, with the Savage at his shoulder.

It was a snap shot; without conscious aim, and in a dusk which wasn't too far from night. Seth Calvert was holding a twelve bore by his hip, and was reloading as fast as he could. Chris aimed for the stock of the twelve bore. The bullet hit its mark, shattered the stock, knocked the gun from the older man's hands, then ricocheted slightly, and scored a bloody path down the outside of Seth Calvert's right thigh.

Seth's howl was a mix of fury and pain. He staggered, righted himself, then made to grab for the broken twelve bore.

Chris was on his feet with the Savage aimed. He snapped, 'Touch it, and I'll send buckshot into your shin.'

They stood, motionless. Each peering at the other through the dusk. Each waiting for the first movement. Seth ready to snatch the twelve bore and, broken stock or not, send the shot into Chris. Chris watching for that slight tensing of the muscles which would prelude that attempt, and ready to shoot buckshot into the elder man's legs.

Two sets of headlights came into view in the distance. They disappeared beyond a rise in the ground, then appeared again, before rounding an outcrop and, finally illuminating the scene in front of the van.

Two vehicles. The battered Daimler and the Ford van. Baxter and Mabel tumbled out of the Daimler. The two under-keepers climbed from the Ford.

Mabel's voice was anxious, as she asked, 'Chris, has he hurt you?'

'No.' Chris kept the Savage levelled.

'He threatened to kill you. To shoot you. I think he meant it.'

'He couldn't wait.' There was the hint of grim humour in Chris's tone. 'He couldn't wait until the door was open.'

Baxter spoke to the under-keepers. 'You two. Take him to a doctor. Get his leg seen to. Then, take him to the police station. Tell Sergeant Rushton. I'll be with him in about an hour. I want him charged. Possibly, Attempted Murder. Certainly Conduct Likely to Cause a Breach of the Peace.' A pause, then, 'And, in future. If you see him on my land, arrest him. Trespass in Pursuit of Game. If he has a gun, shoot him.'

The under-keepers blinked, but didn't argue. They held Seth Calvert by the arms, and hustled him into the rear of the van.

As they drove off, Baxter turned to Chris. 'And you. You need a change of pyjamas, after rolling in the muck. Get a coat on. I'll drive the pair of you to the cottage, before I go to the police station to take care of your uncle.'

Chris muttered, 'He's *not* my bloody uncle.'

'Who the hell he is.'

* * *

A hot bath, freshly laundered pyjamas, a heavy dressing-gown (and that it was Seth Calvert's dressing-gown made it no less cosy) a mug of hot, sweet tea and a freshly-stoked, roaring fire made for a form of earthly paradise, and Chris sat in the wooden-backed armchair and luxuriated.

'He's spoiled everything.' Mabel sat in the companion chair across the hearth rug. She sipped at her own mug of tea. 'I knew he'd spoil it. We had this place, a good job . . . everything. And now he's upset everybody, with his drinking and his temper. And I think Sir Arnold suspects the other thing.'

'You mean his preference for men?'

She nodded, and looked even more miserable. She muttered, 'You won't understand, of course. You're too young.'

'Aunt Mabel . . .' He swallowed, then blurted, 'I understand. I *do* understand. It's an insult. To *you*, I mean.'

'Is that all?' The hint of a smile was very sad.

140

'They tell me it's a disease. That I should feel sorry for him. That he can't help it. I don't think I *want* to understand. It's like the "cities of the plain" in the Bible. Depraved. Filthy.'

It was quite an outburst, and Chris waited until they'd both sipped tea and calmed down, before he spoke.

'I think he knows,' he said gently. 'Sir Arnold, I mean. About Seth and his men friends.'

'I'm so ashamed,' she whispered.

'Don't be.' He leaned forward. Awkward. Wanting to comfort, but not knowing how. He said, 'He offered me post of head keeper. Did you know that?'

'He said.' Then, in a stronger voice, 'That's what made Seth so furious.'

'I refused.'

'Aye. He said that, too. But Seth was convinced you'd gone behind his back.'

'I wouldn't do a thing like that.'

'No. I know you wouldn't, pet. But Seth wouldn't be told.'

There was another short, tea-sipping silence, then Chris spoke in a deliberately off-handed tone.

'I suggested he make *you* head keeper.'

'Eh?' The surprise was such that she slopped a tiny spillage of tea onto the rug.

'You,' repeated Chris.

'Head keeper?'

'Why not? You're at least as good as Seth,

141

and you can handle a gun. You'll stay in the cottage, then.' There was a pause, before he added, 'Maybe mother would like to come and live with you.'

'She has an admirer,' said Mabel, softly. 'Didn't you know?'

'She doesn't write.' The tone was gruff, as if to hide a hurt. 'I don't blame her. I'm a poor one for letter-writing. I don't think I even answered her last two.' Then, 'Anyway ... you could still do it.'

'Oh no.' But the negative dismissal of the idea wasn't quite as uncompromising as before. 'Whoever heard of a woman gamekeeper?'

'Last week—in one of the old copies of *The Field*—I read about a woman shepherd. Out on the fells somewhere. Why not a woman gamekeeper?'

'I don't think Walter and George would accept it for a moment.'

'I'll talk to them,' he promised. 'I know for a fact that *they* don't want it ... they both expect to be in uniform soon. And I think Sir Arnold might like the idea. Say you will ... then leave it to me.'

* * *

It was generally accepted that Walter Wilkins decided all things as far as he and George Henry were concerned. They were both under-

142

keepers. In some vague way, they were related; second-cousins ... something like that. They were both moderately efficient keepers and, for years, they'd been bullied by Seth Calvert.

Chris had sent word for Walter to visit him at the van and, on this day, they were seated, side by side, on the step leading up to the van door.

Chris was saying, 'If there is a war...'

'Oh, there'll be a war.' Walter sounded very certain. 'The major was lecturing us last week. It's coming. And soon. The major was saying—this coalition under Chamberlain only makes it surer. Hitler will run wild. And Mussolini is forever shouting from some balcony. One of them will start a war. Nothing surer.'

'And that's why you don't want the job of head keeper?'

'Eh?'

'Y'know ... now Seth has gone?'

'Oh!' Then, 'It was—y'know—hinted at. Sir Arnold. He hinted at it.'

'And?'

'Well, when the war starts, we're in. Both of us. He'll simply get another head keeper ... then that's us two out. When it's over, I mean.'

'Could be you're right,' said Chris solemnly.

'I am right. It's a bit worrying. Some bugger we don't know gets the job of head keeper, we go off to war, and he puts a couple of his pals in. That's what'll happen. That, for sure.'

143

'If somebody we know took the job...'

'Who? You?'

'No. Not me. Chances are *I'll* be joining up, if there *is* a war.'

'Who, then?'

'Somebody we can all rely on. Somebody who'll make sure the jobs are waiting for us when we get back.'

'Who?'

'Mabel.' Then, hurriedly, 'She can do it, Walt. She's as good at pheasant rearing as any man. She *did* do it, most of the time. When Seth was too drunk to stand upright.'

'I know. But...'

'And she knows us all. She'll keep our jobs for us. You, as head keeper, as likely as not.'

'You think so?'

'Why not? She'd only be a stop-gap. Till the end of the war.'

'It's worth thinking about ... isn't it?'

'Long term. That's what it boils down to.' Chris's voice dropped a little to conspiratorial level. 'Have a word with George. I'm sure he'll agree it's the best long-term solution. We don't want strangers muscling in on our job. We want a firm future, if we can fix it.'

'And Mabel? What if she won't agree?'

Chris smiled and said, 'I'll talk to Mabel. Explain why. She'll see things our way. And I'll drop hints to Sir Arnold, if I get the chance.'

*   *   *

There wasn't much light on the outskirts of Hunslet Moor. No houses, therefore no reflection from lighted windows. A few street gas-lamps, but at least half of them weren't functioning; their mantles had been broken by mischievous kids kicking the post of the lamp, and causing vibration enough to break the thin membrane.

It gloried in the name of 'moor', but it was not a moor as Chris understood that word. It was merely an area of crushed clinker ash, rolled flat and used for football in winter and cricket in summer. The annual Hunslet Feast filled the space with roundabouts, swings, rides and side-shows and, occasionally, some half-hearted 'carnival' took over and tried for some brand of jollity. But it was still Hunslet Moor and smack in the middle of the slum and, after dark, it wasn't too safe.

Chris had followed the man from Anchor Street and now he followed him, silently, along the edge of Hunslet Moor. He'd watched him come from the house. Seen him timidly peck at the cheek of Hetty Calvert at the door. Then he'd followed him at a safe distance; gradually easing himself nearer and nearer to the stranger he intended to kill.

It was both simple and logical. Kill *him*, then his mother Hetty would have no reasonable excuse for not moving house to share a home with Mabel, his aunt. One quick thrust of the knife and all the problems were ended.

Just, that he hadn't expected this traipse along the edge of Hunslet Moor. No matter. It was dark and perhaps even better than the warren of mean streets around his mother's home.

He quickened his pace a little, in order to close up to his intended victim. He eased his jacket aside in order to grasp the knife in its sheath, at his belt. It was a knife he used almost daily; to gut rabbits, to whittle branches, to peel and cut fruit. It was honed to razor sharpness and had a point like a needle.

A voice said, 'Now then, young 'un. D'you mind telling me where *you're* off to at this time?'

Chris jerked his hand from the haft of the knife and spun round to face the police constable who had silently arrived alongside him, riding a pedal cycle.

'Eh! What?'

'You up to summat?' The constable rested both feet on the ground. 'Just *what* are you doing, out at this time?'

'A train,' muttered Chris. 'I'm making my way to the station, to catch a train.'

'Oh, aye? Where to?'

'Pately Bridge.'

'That's a bloody tale, lad.' The constable swung a leg over the saddle of his cycle and stood alongside Chris. 'The last train for *there* left hours ago.'

'The *first* train.' Chris's voice was becoming more certain. 'I've been visiting, and stayed too late. That's why. Missed the last tram, so I have to catch the first train, after walking into town.'

'What's your name, lad?'

'Christmas Calvert. Chris Calvert.'

'And your address?'

'I'm a site gamekeeper on Sir Arnold Baxter's estate.'

'Up north?'

'Yes.'

'And what are you doing here, in this dump?'

'My mother lives here. In Anchor Street.'

'You can prove all this?' questioned the constable.

'Yes.' Chris felt in his inside pocket. 'Letters. A game licence. A driving licence.' He handed the documents to the constable, who examined them in the beam of a torch. He handed the documents back to Chris, hoisted the cycle and turned it to face the way it had come, and said, 'Right, lad. We'll just be sure, shall we? We'll go let your mother know you're out.'

'She'll be in bed.'

'I shouldn't be surprised. We'll knock her up.'

'She won't like that.'

'Lad,' said the constable solemnly, 'I don't give much of a damn what she likes, or what she doesn't like. I'm going to make sure you're who you say you are, before I let you loose.'

'Am I under arrest?'

'Let's say we like each other's company, and it's a dark night, an ungodly hour and we can't bear to be parted.'

*　　　*　　　*

'Why?' asked Hetty Calvert. 'I mean, *why*?'

'I have a right to come and see you, now and again,' mumbled Chris.

'But you *didn't* come to see me. I think that bobby still doesn't quite believe you're my lad.'

'He believes,' grunted Chris. 'He wouldn't have been satisfied if he didn't.'

'All right, then ... *why*?'

She wore a not-very-new overcoat as a makeshift dressing-gown. Her feet were in worn slippers. Her hair was like a crow's nest, with more grey than Chris remembered, and she looked pale and not too healthy. But she also wore a wrist-watch; tiny, mother-of-pearl faced, with a slender leather strap. In all her life, she hadn't had enough money to buy ladies' wrist-watches.

Chris said, 'Right. I'll be getting back. It's a long walk to the station.'

'I want to know why,' she demanded. 'I've a right to know why.'

'Ask your boyfriend,' snarled Chris, with sudden violence. 'And be glad you *can* ask him.'

He turned, stormed out of the house and slammed the door behind him.

148

'And did she?' asked Avril.

'What?'

'Take over as head gamekeeper? After all the cunning and fiddling, did she move into Seth's shoes?'

'No.' Chris almost sighed. He sipped at his whisky and water, then looked slightly bitter; as if the memories were starting to touch tender nerve-ends. 'Baxter wouldn't wear it. He brought a new man in, and Aunt Mabel had to move out. She went to live in the village.' His mouth twisted a little. 'Anyway, it wasn't worth it. George was killed at Dunkirk and Walter was killed somewhere in Europe, after the invasion.'

'And your job?'

'As far as I know, that was there for the asking, after the war. But who the hell wants an on-site gamekeeper's job? Not me. I had better things to do.'

'Of course. Pollard said.'

'Pollard,' said Chris, 'has "said" too much. He always was mouthy.'

They sat at a small, round table, in the lounge of one of the better hotels of the Fylde coast. They had a corner—almost an alcove—to themselves, and the room was almost empty. It would fill up later, but in the

149

main only with locals. This was 'out of season' and the crush of visitors had ended, and wouldn't re-start until the Christmas period.

They'd already ordered dinner. The waiter would visit their table, and tell them when to move into the dining room. Meanwhile, they sipped whisky and sherry, and luxuriated in the warmth of the open fire which blazed a few yards away. It was a large fireplace, and the burning cobs, with short logs on top, hissed and spat as if unwilling to give out their imprisoned heat.

Very sadly, Avril said, 'So much hatred!'

Chris looked a question.

'For Pollard,' she expanded. 'After all these years. The hatred hasn't lessened at all. It's there in your voice.'

'It's there,' he agreed, grimly.

'*Can't* you forgive? Just a little?'

'When he's six foot under,' growled Chris. 'Then I can forget ... but not forgive.'

'I wonder why,' she mused.

1942

In the third floor bedroom at Goy Castle a form of carnal murder was taking place.

Chris had arrived there late afternoon. He'd ripped off his clothes as if they were soiled, then stood under a shower until the near-scalding

150

water had turned his whole body pink.

He'd returned to the bedroom to see Avril there, waiting. She'd straightened the clothes and placed them neatly on a chair.

As he'd climbed into the already-made bed, he'd snarled, 'Take your clothes off. Strip. Everything.'

A little wonderingly, she obeyed, then she'd joined him in bed. And then, in effect, he'd attacked her. The savagery with which he entered her scared her at first. Then her fear had turned to excitement. Then eagerness. And, finally, her fervour matched his. When he climaxed he groaned, as if in pain, then panted as he rolled off her and lay on his back on top of the bed.

They lay there, side by side, staring up at the ceiling of the bedroom. Each carried the sheen of perspiration on their skin. Each breathed heavily.

Avril half-turned and felt on the bedside table near her head. She fumbled two cigarettes from their packet, then thumbed a lighter into flame and lighted the cigarettes. She held one towards him as she spoke.

'Boyo, that's enough lust for a while. Get your breath back, then tell me the reason for the rush of blood to the head. Then when you've got your strength back, we can enjoy some gentle, civilised love-making.'

He waited until he'd enjoyed two deep pulls on the cigarette, then he said, 'Pollard made me

151

kill a dead man.'

'Eh?'

'Hess.'

'Who?'

'Hess ... the man who dropped in by parachute, last...'

'I know who Hess is. And you say Pollard made you kill *him*?'

'He was already dead. The goons had been at him. God knows what they'd done, but he was a hollow man. He didn't know ... *nothing*. Just sat there and let me blow his head apart. And *I* bloody well did it.'

'If you were ordered...'

'Ordered, my arse!' He drew on the cigarette again. 'Can't you understand? They'd pumped too much dope into him. He was a zombie. He didn't know where he was. Who he was. Why he was there. *Nothing*. And Pollard made me vanish the poor sod.'

'There must be a reason.'

'Somebody might see. The International Red Cross. Somebody like that. They might see him, and realise what the bastards have done to him. That's why. Some crap-arsed holier-than-thou thing they want to maintain. And *I've* had to vanish the poor devil for no better reason than that.'

'But what do they hope to gain? Hess arrives here in one piece. Healthy. Even talkative. Then he's dead. That's going to take some explaining when somebody wants to interview the man who was Hitler's deputy. There has to be...'

'There *is*,' interrupted Chris. 'I saw him. I ate with him. Some German goofball who looks remarkably like Hess... but isn't. Oh, he *thinks* he is. He *acts* as if he is. At a guess, he's been brainwashed into *believing* he is. But he's a double. Pollard made that clear. Hess had to be vanished... but still *be* here.'

Avril lay silent for a moment, then said, 'Hess, and his double?'

'That's it.' Chris nodded at the ceiling.

'And you killed Hess?'

'I'm not too proud of it.'

'Or, the other?'

'Eh?'

'Do you *know* Hess? Other than photographs I mean. Do you *know* him?'

'Not personally.'

'Therefore, it could have been the double you vanished?'

'How the hell could it have...' He stopped, and his lips pursed into a silent whistle. His eyes widened and he breathed, 'You're right. You are so damned *right*. That bastard Pollard. *Anything!*'

They booked into the hotel as if they were civilians; man and wife on a quiet holiday, away from the bustle of wartime manufacturing. It was a nice hotel, not too far from Woodhall Spa; way, and gone to hell in the depths of what had already become known as Bomber County. Lincolnshire, base of Number Five Group, Bomber Command. They were Mr and Mrs Lewis, and Avril wore a wedding band to emphasise the fact.

That first afternoon, they walked the nearby lanes in that flattest of all counties. Above them the late spring sky was pale blue and cloudless. If there was a slight chill in the air, it didn't matter. And, endlessly, aero engines formed a background to the gentle noise of the countryside. Avro Ansons and Air Speed Oxfords winged their passengers from one airfield to another. A Battle returning from a drogue-towing detail. An odd Halifax on a cross-country training flight. Occasionally, a Sterling. Now and again, a Wellington from some Air Crew Training Unit. But mostly Avro Lancasters; the workhorse of the heavy-bombing war. Wheeling and turning and changing the pitch of its airscrews, as if defying any of the others to claim so much as a blade of grass from this county, from which it took off to deliver its bomb load to Nazi Germany.

They walked side by side. They might, indeed, have been newly-weds. For perhaps two hours, they forgot the war and their own part in the blood-letting.

They sat on a form to rest, and Avril murmured, 'Skellingthorpe. Where exactly is it? No signposts, no village names. How the hell are we expected to find our way around?'

Chris said, 'We meet him at Woodhall Spa. There's a hotel there. He'll approach *us*.'

'Where does Skellingthorpe come in?'

'There's a drome there. Fifty Squadron and Sixty-One Squadron. That's where His Nibs is stationed. He runs a motor cycle—which must be handy. He can get about a bit.'

'Motor cycle.' Avril smiled and went on, 'Happy days.'

'Eh?'

'Pre-war.'

'You rode a motor cycle?'

'No. A pedal cycle, actually. I went miles, every weekend. Dartmoor. Bodmin Moor. The length and breadth of Cornwall, with much of Devon thrown in. As I say, "Happy days".'

'With some club?' asked Chris.

'Alone.' She seemed to want to talk. Her eyes were slightly dreamy as she continued, 'Father was an officer at Devonport. We lived inland, at a place called Harrowbarrow. Right on the border between the two counties. Handy for the moors and the countryside. Handy for the

155

seaside. I had a great childhood.'

'Why not the Navy?' asked Chris.

'Father was convinced that every sailor, of whatever rank, was a sex maniac. He wouldn't hear of it. The R.A.F. .... serving with perfect gentlemen.'

'He thought *that*?' Chris smiled.

'Chris. There's no bigger fool than a doting parent.'

'I wouldn't know.'

*　　　*　　　*

The boozer had a beer garden. As with every other boozer, there was a limit to the amount of beer available, but the garden was nice. Round tables, made of cast iron, with heavy oak tops. They should have been handed in for the iron collection but, at a guess, the wheels-within-wheels had turned a few times.

Chris and Avril sat at one of the tables. Strictly speaking it wasn't quite warm enough for this sort of caper, but they, and the chubby wing commander they were sharing the table with, were the only people in the garden and at least that ensured privacy.

The wing commander waved his half-empty tankard in the general direction of the car park and said, 'The Norton. The only motor cycle here.'

'All the way from Skellingthorpe?' said Chris.

'Back lanes, my old son.' The wing commander smiled. 'He knows his way. A damned sight better than we in the Provost Marshal's Office do. *And* a souped-up motor cycle. He can take corners at faster speeds than any car.' A pause, then, 'Anyway, we daren't make it too obvious that we're eyeing him over. We want to catch him. Not scare him.'

'But Woodhall Spa?'

'It's the watering hole for a new squadron.' The wing commander tasted his beer, then continued quietly and cautiously. 'It's just been created. This new squadron. Six One Seven Squadron. It's unique. More gongs than seems possible. Every man an old hand at this bombing game.'

'So?' Chris looked puzzled.

'So,' said the wing commander, 'it has to be for something special. Dammit, it's a squadron of heroes. It's there for *something*. Even I don't know what ... but it's worth the Hun keeping an eye on it.'

'And this pillock from Skellingthorpe works for the Hun?' growled Chris.

The wing commander nodded, then said, 'We're ninety per cent sure.'

'Ninety per cent?' murmured Avril.

'I'm told,' said the wing commander coldly, 'that ninety per cent is quite good enough. That's what Pollard tells me.'

'Pollard!' sneered Chris.

'And he gets it from Dansey.'

'What Dansey says ... goes.'

They were silent for a few minutes while the wing commander finished his beer. He placed the empty tankard on the table, pushed himself to his feet and, without speaking again, walked off towards the car park.

*   *   *

The man they'd been ordered to 'vanish' left the side door of the boozer and wandered into the car park. He approached the Norton and, as he gripped the handlebars to haul it off its stand, Chris moved alongside him and pushed the half-hidden muzzle of the .38 service revolver into the man's side.

Chris said, 'This is no joke, friend. This a *real* gun, with *real* bullets.' The man froze into immobility and Chris continued, 'Leave the machine where it is. We're going by car. And be advised. You are the most expendable person north of the Thames.'

The man gawped a little, then croaked, 'Look! I don't know what...'

'We'll tell you,' snapped Chris. He jerked his head. 'Into the car. The engine's running and the lady is waiting.'

'I don't see...'

'You can either walk, or be carried.'

The man nodded miserably and shuffled towards the Austin. He and Chris climbed into the rear seat, Avril engaged the gears, and they

158

left the car park.

Half an hour later, having passed through Horncastle, Greetham and Somersby, they drew into the yard of a broken down, isolated farm. It was obviously unoccupied and, by the look of things, had been unoccupied for years. The windows were gone, much of the roof was missing, the gates were broken and the doors hung drunkenly from damaged hinges.

'Out,' ordered Chris.

Avril killed the engine, then the three of them walked towards the only reasonable building left standing. An old mistal. Chris kept the .38 well in view and the man obeyed instructions without any argument.

Inside the gloom of the mistal, the business of the evening began. Chris motioned with the gun and said, 'On the floor, with your back to the wall.'

'Are you . . .' began the man.

'On the floor, with your back to the wall.'

The man obeyed. The floor dirt and the flaking lime wash made his sergeant's uniform filthy, but nobody seemed to notice.

'You have a transmitter,' said Chris. 'We want to know where it is.'

'I don't know what . . .'

'You're going to tell us. You can either tell us now, or go through agony first.'

'Who the hell *are* you?' The man seemed to gather some sort of courage.

'I,' said Chris, 'am the guy who's going to

159

shoot you. The lady is here to watch and enjoy the performance. The transmitter?'

'Special Branch?'

'The transmitter?'

'You're not the police. They wouldn't...'

'We know it's near here. You've been traced, sonny. Just tell us *where*, and we'll be satisfied.'

'MI5. That's who you are. You're bloody...'

Chris tilted the revolver and squeezed the trigger. It wasn't a magnum. It wasn't even a .45. But in the enclosed space of the mistal, the explosion seemed to make the walls shudder, and sent a scattering of dust from the beams.

The man screamed and snatched at his left wrist with his right hand. It upset his balance a little and he sprawled on the floor. His left hand was mangled where the bullet had smashed into it, and the blood was running in tiny rivulets along the floor. After that first scream, he sobbed with pain as he nursed his wounded hand.

'The transmitter?' said Chris coldly.

'Look!' The man's voice was little more than a croak. 'They've my parents. Both parents. In one of those bloody camps. They'll *die*, if I don't.'

'Don't what?' asked Avril.

'Keep them informed. Y'know ... give them information.'

'The transmitter?' Chris's voice showed complete non-interest in the man's parents, or

160

their predicament.

'I can't. They'll...'

Once more the explosion filled the mistal. More dust fell from the beams, and the man screamed. This time he jack-knifed forward and clutched at his left ankle. The sobbing became a series of deep-throated groans.

Chris said, 'You still have a hand and a leg left. Where's the transmitter?'

'In the...' The man fought to control himself, then gasped, 'In the barn. Under the bin.'

'The bin?'

'The feed bin. Pull it forward, then tip it. It's hidden under the bin.'

Avril said, 'I'll go.'

She left the mistal and the two men waited. The man continued to sob with pain. The impression was that his face had collapsed in upon itself. Tears ran from his eyes, mucus streamed from his nose and spittle left his mouth in a steady dribble. He'd tried to wipe his face dry with his right hand, and left a bloody streak across his features. He was a pitiful sight, but Chris gave no hint of pity. He stood there, motionless, with the revolver tilted towards the suffering man.

Avril returned, carrying a fat, suitcase-like package.

She said, 'It was there. I doubt whether we'd have found it very easily without his help.'

'Get the car started,' said Chris. 'Take the

161

transmitter with you.'

She left and less than a minute later, they heard the car engine cough into life.

The man gasped, 'Do something for me ... *please.*'

Chris said, 'Sure,' and squeezed the trigger, twice.

The first round took the man in the chest and smashed him back into the wall. The second was also a chest shot. It merely made sure. The first round had killed him anyway.

*   *   *

About fifteen minutes later, Avril braked the car to a halt alongside a telephone kiosk. Chris entered the kiosk, fed coins into the box, then dialled a number.

He said, 'B. Squad here. Pass the word. We have what we wanted. There's a collection detail required at the point already identified.'

He left the kiosk, climbed back into the car, and they continued their journey to Woodhall Spa.

1992

'And were they?' asked Avril.
  'Eh?'
  'Never mind. Later.'

They were in the dining room of the hotel. A corner table and with a reasonable space from the other tables. They were the first in there—the 7.30pm sitting—and they were, for the moment, alone. But the waiter was approaching, and he placed the grill dish on a side-table and began boning the Dover sole with smooth expertise.

Chris said, 'Leave the fennel in the dish, please.'

'Yes, sir.'

Two waitresses arrived, one carrying the rack of lamb chops, the other carrying a partitioned dish on which were the vegetables.

'Boiled potatoes, madam?'

'Three please.'

'Beans?'

'Yes, please.'

'Would you care for some tartar sauce, sir?'

'Please. And French fries.'

'Yes, sir.'

'Brussels sprouts, madam?'

'Just a spoonful.'

It was a ritual. It went with the meal. They were paying for it, and it was as important and as expensive as the newly laundered table cloth and the freshly starched napkin. It was civilised eating and it was obvious that both Chris and Avril had grown used to it.

At last, it was over. The white wine had been uncorked, tasted, poured and the bottle settled into an ice bucket. All the waiters had left and, once more, they had complete privacy.

Avril loaded her fork and said, 'I was asking. Were they?'

'Who? What?'

'The man's parents. *Did* they die? *Were* they killed?'

'God knows.' Chris lifted a tasting of sole to his mouth, chewed, then said, '*He* died. That was the limit of our mandate.'

'You still don't care?' She sounded surprised. Perhaps even slightly shocked.

'The first Dam Buster's raid. We didn't know it then, of course. But if the Hun had known ... If the bastard had found out, and transmitted *that* information ... It was a dicey enough operation, as it was.'

She nodded, as if partly convinced. They ate in silence for all of two minutes, before she spoke again.

Very softly, she said, 'That was then I started being scared of you.'

'Eh?' He looked up.

'Scared of you,' she repeated.

'You were never scared of me.' He chuckled quietly. 'You were never scared of *anything*.'

'And don't ever believe *that*,' she said solemnly.

For most of the rest of the meal they remained silent. Avril was eating chocolate gateau and cream, and Chris was sipping coffee and eating cheese and biscuits before either of them broke the silence.

164

Avril said, 'Had you asked me, I might have married you . . . before the Dam Buster's raid.'

'Had I asked you,' said Chris sourly.

'I counted you as being human, until then.'

'I was human. I'm still human. My profession demands that I keep a tight rein on my emotions.'

'You do an excellent job of it.'

'*I* think so.' Chris sipped coffee then went on, 'Have you ever wondered why Pollard never arranged *your* demise?'

'Why should he?' She blinked her surprise.

'It was his job. Ensuring that various people "vanished". He was good at it. I suspect he enjoyed his work.'

'It was necessary.'

'Was it?' Chris popped a piece of cheese into his mouth.

'There was always a reason.'

'Of course. Sometimes a very private reason.'

1938

May. The time for dancing on village greens. The time of green buds and a promise of new life. An 'awakening' time. A new time, a clean time, a joyful time . . . but this year, it wasn't.

The Austrian Corporal had annexed his homeland as an extension of Germany and, as

165

all but the blind could see, something nasty was brewing up on the continent of Europe.

The weather on the exposed moors seemed to catch onto the general foulness. Heavy morning dew followed by an overall dullness and an almost continual drizzle. And on this morning Chris, Jared and Morven Smith sat in the shelter of the gypsy van and watched the rain systematically soak the world. The boys were in the tent. The lurchers were under the van. The horse was in what little shelter the tarpaulin lean-to could provide.

'It's set in,' said Chris. 'It's here for the day.'

'We could do with warmth,' observed Morven.

'I hear our kind are getting more than warmth over in Germany.' Jared's words were meant as a criticism to his wife's complaining.

'The Jews,' said Chris.

'Aye, and the travelling people. Hitler don't like the Romany people.'

'I hear tell there's likely to be a war.'

Jared grunted, but said nothing.

'If there *is* a war,' said Chris, 'will you be joining up?'

'I couldn't live inside.' It was a soft-spoken, end-of-argument remark. There was a silence, then, 'Will you?'

'I reckon.'

'Why?'

'I can shoot. That's all war boils down to.'

They watched the dark, rippling water of the

tarn, and each remained silent with personal thoughts for all of two minutes then, at her position by Chris's ankles, Queenie stiffened and began to push herself upright.

Chris murmured, 'Easy, girl,' and the dog relaxed a little.

From beneath the van they heard the low growl from the lurchers.

'Somebody's around,' said Jared softly.

Chris hefted the Savage under-and-over into a slightly more comfortable position across his knees, then all three of them strained their hearing in an attempt to catch some slight sound of movement above the faint hiss of the steady downpour.

They heard heavy breathing, then Seth Calvert weaved his way around the side of the van and came into view. He was outrageously drunk. He was also soaked to the skin. He had no coat and no hat and his shirt, beneath his braces, clung to his thick body like a wet membrane. He stared short-sightedly up at the occupants of the van, and swayed a little as he spoke.

He slurred, 'I thought I'd find thi wi' thi tinker friends.'

Jared tightened his muscles and Chris touched him, warningly.

Chris said, 'I like Romany company. I *don't* like drunks.'

'Aaah!' Seth waved a dismissive hand, then said, 'I want my job back.'

167

'I can't help you there ... even if I wanted to.'

'Oh, aye. You can.'

'No.'

'Sir Arnold thinks the sun shines out of your arse, lad. You know that...'

'No.'

'A few words. That's all.'

'No.'

'I want my job back.'

'I can't help you.'

'*Won't* help me.'

'Could be.'

'I want my job back.' Seth swayed and almost fell. 'I want the bloody cottage back. It's *mine.*'

'Move.' Chris raised the Savage and allowed his finger to move towards the trigger. 'You're trespassing, and Sir Arnold warned you. We can also do without your company.'

'You—you wouldn't bloody *dare.*'

'Don't put money on that belief, Seth Calvert.' The voice was cold and without even the hint of mercy.

'By God!' Seth stared drunkenly for a moment, then muttered, 'You *would,* an' all.'

'Oh yes.' Chris nodded. 'And enjoy doing it.'

As the finger strayed nearer to the trigger, Seth Calvert backed away, then turned and ran, drunkenly, towards the shelter of a small hillock.

Jared said, 'Take care, friend. That one knows how to hate.'

'Drink makes a dwarf think he's a giant,' said Chris dismissively.

* * *

More than an hour later Chris left the Smiths' site and made his way towards his own van. It was still raining, but the drizzle had turned into stair-rod downpours which seemed to ride on the gusts of growing wind. Chris wore a heavy, oilskin slicker, under which he carried the Savage. The dog—utterly soaked—trotted at his heel.

They dropped into a slight dip before the climb to the van, and he almost fell over the sprawling, legs-spreadeagled Seth. He had obviously stumbled in his drunken condition and seemed almost to be under the water in the lashing rain.

Chris paused, but only for a moment. He growled, 'Leave him, girl,' to the dog, and continued his journey home.

In the van he rubbed the dog dry with clean sacking, removed his own wet clothes, fired the stove, brewed tea then made himself a cold beef sandwich. It was still pouring, so he settled himself in the armchair to read.

* * *

At first light next morning, the rain had stopped. Chris opened the van door to allow

169

Queenie out, and heard the distant shouts of the search party. They were not within sight of the van, but he knew his area well enough to guess that they'd find Seth Calvert in a short time.

He breakfasted, then left the van to patrol in a direction which took him well away from the search party.

He returned to the van at early evening. The donkey cart was there, and so was Mabel.

She followed him into the van before she spoke more than the necessary greeting.

Then she said, 'Seth's dead.'

'Oh!' He pretended surprise.

'Jared Smith says you saw him yesterday.'

'Yes.' Chris nodded. 'He was drunk. I warned him off the land.'

'Jared says.'

'He was trespassing, and Sir Arnold insists that he keeps off the estate.'

'Of course.' There was no criticism in her tone. She continued, 'He was drunk. Very drunk. He must have fallen asleep and slept the night away, in the rain.'

'Oh!'

'We found him this morning.'

'Dead?'

'No. Not dead. But in a bad way. We took him to the cottage hospital. It was a combination of exposure and pneumonia. He didn't regain consciousness. Not really.'

Chris said, 'I'm sorry,' and lied.

'Don't be.' Then, sombrely and quietly, 'He wasn't worth tears. He isn't worth tears, now.'

Chris filled the kettle and said, 'You'll be staying in the cottage?' He made it into a question.

'I reckon.' Her smile was touched with whimsical sadness. 'Sir Arnold says I can ... until things have been sorted out.'

*   *   *

They buried Seth Calvert five days later. In the yard of the village church, where tombstones leaned drunkenly in every direction.

Hetty visited for the funeral. The two under-keepers attended, with two women servants from the hall. There was also a thin, wan-faced man, with white hair, a dark suit and well-polished shoes. He cried openly as the vicar intoned the requisite words and the grave-diggers lowered the coffin.

All the other mourners ignored the man, but he didn't seem to mind. When the service was over and the others wandered from the grave, he stayed behind, gazed at the lid of the coffin, then bent, picked up a small handful of earth and threw it into the hole. He did it in a manner which was almost holy.

171

'Robertson is dead.' Pollard faced the four members of B Squad and passed the news of the death of their colleague, as if he was making a passing remark about the weather. He continued, 'As you know, he always worked with D'Souza, and the shock has been a little too much for her. She's on indefinite compassionate leave.'

Chris asked, 'How was he killed?'

'Eh?' Pollard looked surprised at the question, as if the death of one of their number was not important enough to have questions attached.

'Robertson. Who killed him?'

'Hit and run,' said Pollard abruptly. 'Last night. Wandering around Aberfeldy in the blackout.'

'And D'Souza?'

'On leave. Sick leave. Compassionate leave.' There was a dismissive tone in his voice as he continued, 'Teale and Wisby ... it's home ground for you. The southern counties. You'll move in with what's left of A Squad. Take Morton with you. There's a big build-up of activity down there. Those who shouldn't know are getting very nosy.'

He turned to Chris and went on, 'You're for France, Calvert. Caen, to be precise. On your own, this time. There's a map to be picked up. A very important map. And it has to be brought out as soon as possible ... if we've to kill a dozen Nazi bastards to get it out.'

*   *   *

Two days after the briefing he'd sat huddled in what small shelter he could find behind the bulwark of a tiny dinghy, as it chugged a silent way past the Le Havre point and into the bay. He was queasy from the crossing, and the two Naval types who manned the craft either hadn't anything worth saying, or were under strict instructions to keep things to themselves. They grounded the boat near Cabourg, then left him alone on the shingle to await the next stage in this very personal invasion of Europe.

A voice whispered, 'It is cold for the time of year, monsieur.'

'Eh?' He jerked his head to where the voice had seemed to come, then whispered back, 'A black frost before morning, I think.'

'Come.' The youngish man, with only one arm, had appeared out of the murk. He'd grasped Chris by the elbow, then led him to a dirt road parallel with the shore; to where two slightly ancient bicycles were waiting under a tree. They rode, south west, towards Caen. Other than the tiny lights on the cycles, they had only the illumination from a moon with a cloud-rack like a tar-scrape.

The one-armed man talked as they rode. Perhaps it was his way of keeping up their spirits. Perhaps he was naturally garrulous. For whatever reason, he talked.

'When we get nearer our destination, monsieur. I have bandages. Bloodied and soiled. We will fit them over your jaw.'

'What? Why the hell...'

'Later, we are likely to be stopped. You have your documents...'

'Of course.'

'The colonel will have seen to that. But—forgive me if I'm wrong—you speak neither French nor German?'

'Only English.'

'You see.' There was a quick flash of teeth in the moonlight. 'With a smashed jaw, it does not matter. Silence is expected. I will do the talking.'

'Oh!'

'Later,' said the one-armed man comfortingly. 'This stretch of coast is Dansey country.'

'Do the Germans know that?' asked Chris in a slightly sour tone.

'The Germans,' said the one-armed man solemnly, 'are children at the spying game.'

'Oh!'

'The British have the MI6, and part of the MI6 is Dansey's Z Organisation. *Us*, monsieur. We are the colonel's eyes and ears.'

'He tends to be alphabetically inclined,'
174

murmured Chris.

'Monsieur?'

'It doesn't matter.' Then, 'I'm told I have to pick up a map.'

'A map,' agreed the one-armed man. 'To be taken back to the colonel as soon as possible. It is all arranged.'

'Why don't you—one of this Z Organisation—take the map to England?'

'We are family,' chuckled the one-armed man. 'The Hun—even the Gestapo—know us. If we left—even one of us—it might spell danger for the rest. The Hun trusts us, and we must ensure he continues to trust us.'

'*Trusts* you!'

'Ah yes, monsieur.' Again the quick flash of teeth. 'We feed him information. Information he thinks he wants. Information we wish him to have. It is—what you call checks and balances.'

'Dangerous,' suggested Chris.

'A little.' The one-armed man shrugged. 'But you see, monsieur, the Hun wishes to be loved. To be popular. He cannot see why we do not welcome him with open arms when he invades our country. It is his weakness and our strength.'

They cycled west, then south and, with dawn not too far away, they stopped at an isolated farmhouse. They fed on coarse bread and strong wine, while women who were obviously experts at the job fitted soiled bandages around the lower half of his face and jaw. They smeared blood around some of the grubby bandage. Chris scowled his displeasure, and the one-armed man grinned and said, 'Pig's blood, monsieur. It will do no harm, and it looks very lifelike.'

Then, when it was almost time to leave, one of the women stepped up and poured a tin jug of evil-smelling liquid over the front of Chris's trousers.

'Cow's pee,' said the one-armed man, before Chris had time to object. 'The Hun considers himself to be fastidious. What you call— incontinence, I think—it makes him screw up his nose in disgust.'

'It makes *me* screw up my nose in disgust,' growled Chris.

'Ah, but they will keep their distance, my friend. That is the reason. To them, you are a disgusting creature, to be given as wide a berth as possible.'

*　　　*　　　*

They entered Caen from the south-east. Via the Boulevard de la Prairie. They dismounted and pushed their cycles along the Avenue Sorel and, as they trudged towards the Place Fontette, a sleepy, uniformed German guard stopped them. There was an exchange between the one-armed man and the guard; an amicable enough exchange and, as forecast, the guard eyed Chris, with his stained trousers and bandaged head, with open disgust.

It was the first uniformed German Chris had ever seen; complete with battle-grey uniform, chamber-pot steel helmet and shoulder-slung sub-machine-gun. It was perhaps a little disconcerting, but the one-armed man chatted away and, apart from a quick look of utter disgust, the enemy ignored the assassin in his midst.

He was slightly surprised to realise that he felt no panic. The uniformed enemy was the personification of all he'd been trained to hate and fear.

The man looked so ordinary. Well-fed, perhaps. Slightly slow-witted if his actions as a guard meant anything. But 'the enemy'—an official representative of Adolf Hitler ... and a not too perfect specimen of manhood, Aryan or not.

*   *   *

He spent the day in the crypt of the Abbaye aux Hommes. He was allowed to bath and shave, and he was provided with fresh clothes. He slept on a narrow, iron bed with a thin mattress and a single Army blanket.

He was awakened in order to eat more coarse bread and drink more wine, then a woman entered the crypt and it was obvious that she enjoyed some standing within the

177

group.

'Marie-Madeleine,' she introduced herself. 'The colonel told you. Yes? There is a map.'

'A map,' he nodded.

'One of our friends—Maurice Dounin—has drawn it. He is an art teacher at the *lycée*. A good man. The colonel requires it as soon as possible.'

'A map?' repeated Chris.

'The coast, monsieur. From Dives to the Cotentin Peninsular. Gun emplacements, strong points, obstacles. Without that map, the Hun can be ready for an invasion. The Allies will be thrown back into the sea.'

'That important?' Chris was impressed.

'Get it back to the colonel, please,' she pleaded. 'Lives have been risked for it. We wish the Allies to succeed.'

* * *

If you take the Boulevard Bertrand, having skirted the back of the Town Hall, at Caen, you will, if you know the back streets, end up at the racecourse. By a short, but devious route it is then fairly easy to reach the River Orne. Then, if the sentry is occupied, arguing with slightly drunken civilians, it is possible to slip across the bridge and hide in a shadowed recess on the Quai Hamelin.

Chris crouched in one of those recesses and watched the road which led to the bridge. A three-inch-wide cylinder was strapped firmly to his back; almost a foot long and sealed at both ends.

As she'd tightened the straps Marie-Madeline had said, 'Get it to the colonel, monsieur. If not, break the top seal. It will self-destruct.'

'And me, with it,' Chris had growled.

'We make sacrifices, monsieur. All of us. But get it to the colonel.' Then she'd leaned forward and kissed him gently on the lips.

And now he was waiting, as if on the start-line of a long and gruelling race. The Luger Parabellum pistol was nicely balanced in his hand, and his eyes had grown accustomed to the darkness.

He worried a little. The teenager who'd guided him from the Abbaye aux Hommes had disappeared into the darkness; back from whence they'd come. That he was alone didn't worry him. That he didn't know Caen nor, other than the general direction, where the French coast lay. Any slip-ups and he'd be left, high and dry, to self-destroy the cylinder and, at the same time, self-destroy himself.

From across the town he heard the quarter chime, then a silence, then the expected explosion. From the direction of the castle, even though it was almost a mile away, the thud seemed to make the cobbles under his feet tremble.

Lights went on, the guard left the bridge at a

run and general activity built up.

At the same time, the motor cycle roared from the Rue de Falaise, turned right into the Quai Hamelin and braked to a halt. Chris left his shadow, swung himself onto the pillion and gripped the rider around the waist. Then off, right into the Rue de la Gare, left along the Rue d'Auge and away from the town.

He'd rammed the Luger into his waist-band as he'd straddled the pillion seat, and now he worried. Had he, or had he not slipped the safety catch on? The ride was slightly hair-raising, merely as a means of locomotion. With a self-destruction mechanism on his back, and a loaded pistol aimed at his groin he figured himself to be in a particularly dangerous position. But a position he could do nothing about.

The motor-cyclist knew the way. He knew every turn and every twist in the back lanes. The only light was from the sky—black silhouettes, from which the motor cycle bounced echoes, hardly distinguishable from the blue-black of the night sky. But the rider leaned into the corners and Chris knew that no mere motor car could take the bends at that speed.

Suddenly, almost unexpectedly, they were racing along the coast road. Then they were slithering through dunes. Finally they reached firmer sand and raced along the water's edge.

The motor cycle spun sand as the rider

braked and, through the gloom, Chris saw the outline of a dinghy, similar to the one he'd arrived in.

A cockney voice hissed, 'As soon as you like, mate.'

The motor cyclist said, 'Good luck, monsieur,' in a remarkably calm voice.

Chris checked the Luger and at a crouch ran through the shallows towards the waiting dinghy, climbed aboard and as the second occupant gunned the outboard motor he was hauled from the sea. Less than five minutes later he was scrambling up the netting of an Air Sea Rescue launch.

Safe in the cabin of the launch, the delayed shock took over. The trembling. The teeth-chattering. The feeling of icy coldness.

'A rough time?' asked an anxious warrant officer.

'Easy,' muttered Chris. '*Too* easy. I hadn't the gumption to realise what I was doing. Where I was.'

'Rum.' The warrant officer held out a tiny glass. 'Good stuff. Being afloat has its compensations.'

*　　　*　　　*

That same evening in an office in London, the monocled Dansey fed Chris canapés topped with caviare, and showed him the map. Fifty-five feet long. Detailed to the last German gun emplacement and camp.

'Worth its weight in diamonds,' said a delighted Dansey.

'Yes, sir.'

'Take a few days' leave. A week. See the town, before you go back up north.'

'Yes, sir.'

*   *   *

Goy Castle offered comparative peace after the big city; after laughing at Sid Field in *Strike a New Note*; after hearing the massed male voice choir of the Red Army; after The Windmill, the night clubs and the girlie-girlie shows; after the sight of gap-toothed bomb damage, sandbags and anti-aircraft batteries.

The towering, castellated walls. The swoop of the surrounding hills; pine-covered and mysterious as they held the magnificent building in a saucer of their slopes.

It was almost a homecoming, and as he entered his bedroom he was surprised to find Avril relaxing on the bed.

As he entered the room she swung herself upright and said, 'Thank God.'

'Eh?' Chris heaved his haversack onto the vacated bed.

'That you're back.'

'Why? What's up? I thought you were down on the south coast with...'

'They're dead.'

182

'What?'

'Teale and Wisby. Both dead.'

'How the hell did that...'

'Beachy Head. They were seeking seagulls' eggs.'

'Seagulls' eggs?' Chris stared.

'Something of a delicacy. They fancied a try. One of them slipped. Pulled the other down with him.'

'And they're both dead?' He flopped into an armchair as he asked the question.

'Both,' she answered shortly. 'Pollard saw it happen. He's still down there, waiting to give evidence at the inquest.'

'Is he?' Chris chewed his lower lip in silence, then said, 'That's three of us gone. Four counting D'Souza. That means...'

'I called to see her,' interrupted Avril.

'What?'

'I called at the private hospital— Harrogate—on my way north. To see her.'

'And?'

'She's pregnant. That's why she's in there.'

'Oh!' Chris scowled, then muttered, 'And Robertson's dead, so...'

'Robertson wasn't the father.'

'I thought...'

'I know. So did I. But it's not Robertson. She's quite sure. And she's very scared.'

'Scared?'

'Pollard's the father. She's been playing both ends off against the middle, and now she's

183

going to have a bambino, but no husband.'

'Does Pollard know?'

'Oh, yes. He's known from the "off".'

'How can she be sure?'

'She's sure. She hasn't the ghost of a doubt. Pollard's the father.'

There was a silence. Chris stared at the carpet with frowning concentration. Avril gazed from the window and, without really seeing them, saw two scratch teams of soldiers playing hockey on the pitch alongside the castle.

In a soft, faraway voice Chris remarked, 'Two of us left. Just us two. The other four have gone. "Vanished". How long before we're no longer around?'

1992

'And neither of us tumbled.'

Christmas Calvert's voice was heavy with self-disgust as he mouthed the words.

They'd entered the Sealife Centre to be out of the weather. They were surrounded by glass and behind the glass swam congers and rays, squids and plaice.

'Why should we?'

She strolled alongside him and, with him, paused to stare back at the staring fish. It was an impossible world; still, yet full of moving

184

shapes; dim, but a mass of strange colours; underwater, but perfectly dry.

'First Robertson. Then Teale and Wisby. D'Souza in a nursing home.' He blew out his cheeks. 'Half of us gone west—more than half out of action—and we were dumb enough to accept it as "normal".'

'We knew something was wrong,' she protested. 'We *knew*. We just didn't know what.'

They strolled into the entrance of a tunnel. A tunnel with glass walls and a glass top; a tunnel which was part of a massive tank, and in which white-bellied sharks, with black-button eyes and grinning, rat-trap mouths, swam effortlessly alongside them and above them. They were sleek, streamlined and very dangerous.

She said, 'What if this glass breaks?'

'We don't have fish for dinner any more. The fish have us.'

They found a lounge; a strange, silent, out-of-this-world lounge, surrounded on all sides by inch-thick glass, behind which swam creatures from the deep. The chairs and the couch were comfortable and, for a few moments, they relaxed in contemplative silence.

Quite suddenly she said, 'Before the Syrian ... what?'

He looked puzzled for a moment, then gave a quick, cold smile and said, 'Before the Syrian

'... nothing.'

'Not even a suspicion?'

'Had you?'

'I had no reason to suspect,' she said. 'We were encouraged to keep within our own group. Even within our separate twosome.' She paused, then continued, 'In those days, I was quite taken with you.' He grunted and she continued, 'I thought I could hear wedding bells. The patter of tiny feet. That sort of thing.' In a slightly dreamy voice, she ended, 'A dream of civilian life. Roses round the door. That sort of thing.'

'But then came the Syrian,' he growled.

'Then came the Syrian,' she agreed. 'And all the swans turned to ducks, and all the gold bricks turned to lead ingots. We both grew up, and at breakneck speed.'

1946

The war had been over more than three months. Nuremberg had seen the farce of a pseudo criminal trial which had no true foundation in law. The bottom line had been drawn under that even greater farce known to the world as the League of Nations.

April '46 ... and in an upstairs room of Goy Castle, Pilot Officer Avril Morton was expressing harsh opinions.

186

'It's over,' she snapped. 'Everybody has come to their senses. Germany's finished. Hitler's killed himself. We don't *have* to go out on some ridiculous limb any more.'

'We're still in the RAF,' growled Chris. 'We can't disobey orders.'

'He's not one of the enemy. We *haven't* any "enemies" now. The war's already history.'

'He's one of the big wheels in just about every black market racket going. Food coupons. Petrol coupons. Booze. Clothes coupons. The lot.'

'Oh, come *on!*' Her eyes blazed. 'Grow up, lover boy. You think Dansey's not feeding his face, every day, at some class West End restaurant? You think Bond Street doesn't make his suits? That he moves around on a bicycle?' She snorted. 'Him, and every member of the War Cabinet. Out there in the sticks ... they drop a pig. A sheep. Even a cow. Who the hell knows? Who the hell *cares?*'

'We obey orders,' insisted Chris.

'Balls,' she snapped, in a very unladylike tone.

'*I* obey orders,' he corrected himself. 'Pollard orders me. He gets *his* orders from Dansey. I do what I'm told.'

'We no longer kill Germans,' she argued. 'They're the vanquished. They *weren't* all Nazis. They *didn't* butcher Jews. They're no longer the enemy.'

'Now who's talking balls?' He gave a

lopsided grin and added, 'Anyway, he's not a German. He's a Syrian.'

'A *Syrian*?' Her glare intensified.

'That's what Pollard tells me.'

'God Almighty!' she exploded, 'Syria wasn't even in the bloody war.'

'That doesn't matter. According to Pollard...'

'Pollard's leading you on. Why the hell should *he* worry about super-spivs and the black market? Even his uniform is made of flash material. He can't...'

'Dansey gives him orders. *He* passes them on. It's not *too* complicated ... surely.'

The glare quietened and she blew out her cheeks in final defeat.

Chris watched with the ghost of a grin on his face. At last she quietened her heated attitude, and her voice carried a near-pleading tone as she continued.

'Chris, don't do this one. Make an excuse. Go sick, anything. Just don't do it.'

'Why?'

'I have a bad feeling ... that's all.'

'You don't like Pollard.'

'Neither of us like Pollard. But it's more than that. It has a bad fishy stench about it.'

'That's because he'll be fishing,' smiled Chris.

'What?'

'His sport. Fishing. That's what he'll be doing when I "vanish" him. Well north of here.

On the Spey.'

* * *

Before emptying itself into Spey Bay, the river raced through some of the wildest country this side of Outer Mongolia. It was the fastest flowing river in Scotland—maybe in the United Kingdom. It was also one of the great salmon rivers of Europe. It smashed its way around rocks. It narrowed to slice ravines through hillsides. It widened to form a flat, deadly, fast-flowing sheet of smoothness with eddies, pools and backwaters, where twenty-five-to-thirty-pounders lurked, ready to do battle. Game fish, waiting for men and women worthy of their mettle. It needed strength, skill and courage to fish the Spey. The running water tried to drag you in, the cold tried to freeze you into immobility and the wind tried to push you under. But if you could fight, and if you could fish, the rewards were often worth it.

Chris lay on his belly behind the cattle wire, on top of a sixty-foot cliff, and watched the man he was there to kill. The range was easy; little more than fifty yards. But a steep, down-sloping shot and a gale force wind that blustered crazily, and a target that continually swayed against the push of the wind and water, didn't make for a quick snapshot.

The man—the Syrian—was wearing waders up to his armpits, in water which was waist-

189

deep. He moved slowly and purposefully, and flicked the line with a skill which mastered both current and wind.

Chris watched and admired while, at the same time, estimating distance and varying wind velocity. He eased the Luger up, from by his side to nearer his shoulder. For a moment the front sight snagged on exposed wool of the fleece-lined flying jacket he was wearing. He half-turned to free it, and saw Pollard, blackjack raised to strike.

Chris half-rolled and fended off the descending blackjack with his left arm. He grabbed Pollard's wrist with his right hand and scissored his thighs with his legs. Pollard came down, and they wrestled with each other on the damp grass.

Chris heaved himself on top of his opponent, held him down with knees in the guts and a left forearm across the throat, while he grabbed for a weapon inside the flying jacket.

He thrust the muzzle into Pollard's gasping mouth, then yelled above the howl of the wind. 'Give me the excuse ... that's all. You'll have wall-to-wall lead where your brains are.'

He meant it, and Pollard knew that he meant it. All resistance stopped abruptly. Pollard froze and, still keeping the Luger trained on Pollard's face, Chris slowly straightened.

He warned, 'Stay there. Don't even *breathe* too heavily,' but he had to almost shout to make himself heard above the wind.

He moved the Luger's snout in a tiny gesture, and said, 'Up ... and slowly.'

Pollard pushed himself to his feet.

'Hands behind the neck,' ordered Chris.

Pollard obeyed and as he did so, said, 'Your demob papers are through.'

'Eh?' Chris didn't understand.

'Your demobilisation papers. And the cheque. They're waiting at the Admin Office at Goy. Collect them. Forget this, and we'll both walk away from each other. Out of each other's lives.'

'Turn round,' snapped Chris.

'It won't do you any good. You won't get away with it.' And if there was the hint of a pleading quality about the tone, it was a mere gossamer touch.

'Turn around,' repeated Chris.

'Why?' And now the words rode on open contempt. 'Haven't you the stomach to watch my face as you shoot me?'

'And smile while I'm doing it,' answered Chris coldly. 'If you think otherwise, you've never been more wrong.'

Pollard nodded, then said, 'One last favour. Kill the Syrian first.'

'Why?' Chris was mildly intrigued.

'A personal favour.'

'Why couldn't *you* have killed him?'

'Kill him,' pleaded Pollard. 'Kill the bastard. A last favour.'

'Why?'

'He's likely to marry D'Souza.'

'So?'

'The child. My daughter. I don't want another man to be her father.'

'Why couldn't *you* have killed him?' repeated Calvert.

'The blame would have been yours. On the face of things, *you* killed him, then fell from the cliff.'

'And you?'

'I'm not here, boy.' Pollard gave the impression that he was resigned to his fate. He said, 'Just a last favour. Kill him.'

Calvert studied the other man for a moment, then said, 'Dansey. Does *he* know about this?'

'Does it matter?'

'To me.'

'You suddenly getting a conscience?' sneered Pollard.

'Something like that.'

'*Nothing* like that, boy,' mocked Pollard. 'You kill when you're told to kill. It's a kink you have. It's why you were chosen. Kill crazy ... that's you, boy. That's *all* of you. That's why you all ended up in the Button Squad. Dansey's bloody darlings ... but what happens when the war's over, and we turn the animals loose?'

'Is that what you think?'

'That's what I *know*.'

They glared bottomless contempt at each other for half a dozen heartbeats, then Calvert

192

moved, smoothly and swiftly.

He stepped a pace nearer, then suddenly raised the pistol and smashed it against Pollard's temple. As Pollard buckled, Calvert pushed the pistol back under the flying jacket. Pollard was not quite unconscious as Calvert hauled him to his feet, hoiked him to the cattle wire and tipped him over the lip. The semi-conscious man sprawled on the rocks, sixty-feet beneath. He lay still. Smashed. Broken. Probably dead. Calvert spared him a quick, uninterested glance, before he picked up the blackjack and the rifle, and walked from the scene.

*　　　*　　　*

It was easy. Ridiculously easy. He arrived at Goy Castle a little after dark, went to his room and, watched by a silent Avril, packed all his clothes and belongings into a suitcase and a kit-bag. He'd packed the Savage, the swordstick and the blackjack into a fishing-rod bag, and had carefully holstered the Luger in a shoulder holster. He'd visited the Orderly Room and, as Pollard had promised, his demobilisation papers were ready for collection. A nice fat cheque. An Identity Card. A brand new Ration Book. Everything ready for handing over against signature.

The Orderly Room Sergeant had said, 'That's it then, sir. You're a civilian again now, sir.'

'I don't feel much difference.'

'You will. Given time, you will.'

And now he was bidding farewell to Avril.

He said, 'I'm taking the car. Tell them at the Motor Pool. I'll leave it with the Transport Office people at Leeds station.'

'I'll let them know.'

She waited expectantly.

He held out his hand and said, 'I'll be on my way, then. We'll maybe meet up again, sometime.'

'Just like that?' Incredulity widened her eyes.

'Eh?'

'Just shake hands? A quick goodbye ... and that's *it*?'

'What else?' He frowned non-understanding. 'We've had some good times—enjoyed each other's company ... but you're not due for demob yet ... or *are* you?'

'Not yet,' she said, tightly.

'Well, then. Chances are we'll meet up again ... sometime.'

They shook hands; he with a firm grip, she with a limp and flaccid gesture that was quite meaningless.

He left and, before he'd reached the car, she allowed herself to weep.

*   *   *

They met again six weeks later. It was in the

early evening and Chris returned to the van to find her waiting for him.

She stood up from the chair as he entered the van.

He stared for a moment, then closed the van door and said, 'I didn't expect to see...'

'This isn't a social call,' she interrupted.

'Oh!'

'Just that Pollard asked me for your home address.'

'Ah!'

'He's gunning for you, boy.' Then, as if she was reluctant to ask, 'What happened at the Spey?'

'He tried to kill me,' said Chris in a toneless voice. 'Instead, I killed him ... or *meant* to.'

'He's still alive. Battered. Broken bones. He'll be on his back for a few more weeks, but he wanted your address.'

'Did you give it to him?'

'No. I said I didn't know.'

'Thanks.'

'But, like me, when he's capable, he can get it from your records.'

'Of course.'

Chris still carried the Savage under his arm. He emptied the chamber, then lifted the rifle to above the van door, where it was housed on two hooks. He filled the kettle from the large, copper water can on a shelf in a corner of the van. He placed the kettle on a gas ring, fed by bottled gas, struck a match to light the flame,

195

then spoke.

'What's your reason for coming here?'

'To warn you.'

'Warn me?'

'I don't want to see you dead.'

'You think he will?'

'It's *Pollard* we're talking about.'

'Pollard never killed anybody ... did he? He was a conduit for Dansey.'

'He was going to kill *you*.'

'Ah!'

'Like he killed Robertson ...'

'You think he ...'

'... and Teale and Wisby.'

'Oh, come *on*!' But the objection was without weight. He paused, then added, 'You really think he did?' Then he frowned and, as if talking to himself, muttered, 'Damn! And I know why.'

'Why?' asked Avril.

'The war's finished. It was as good as finished when Robertson went.'

'So?'

'Turning the animals loose. That's what he said ... just before I pushed him over the cliff. Dansey's idea. Bet on it. Shift us. We've done what we were meant to do, so now eliminate us before it's too late.'

'Too late for what?'

Instead of answering the question, Chris asked, 'Where is he?'

'Who?'

'Pollard, of course.'

'Oh, no.' She shook her head. 'I don't want to see *him* killed, either.'

'No. Of course not. You're not one of us. Not really. You were there to keep me amused...'

'That's a lousy thing to...'

'Teale and Wisby kept each other amused, and D'Souza was there to keep Robertson amused. Like a jigsaw puzzle. Each piece fits into the other. And now the jigsaw's finished with, the pieces are thrown away.'

'What the hell are you trying to say?' snapped Avril.

'This war we've just fought.' Chris turned to stare out of the window. In a musing voice he continued, 'We deported ourselves like perfect English gentlemen. That's what the public think. The Hun did everything bad. We did nothing but good.' He paused, sighed, then said, 'I wonder what history will say. When the nasty little secrets leak out. Secrets like us. The men and women who were killed, merely because they were something of a nuisance. The killers who slaughtered from the shadows. *Us*. What will history say about *us*?'

She blew out her cheeks and said, 'Boy ... you certainly hate yourself.' She stood up from the chair and said, 'Well, that's it. I've warned you. That's why I came. The van brought me out from the house. It's waiting to take me back to the station.'

'I thought...' began Chris.

'What?'

'A cup of tea, maybe. Something to...'

'No.' Then in a quiet, tight voice, 'No tea, thank you. I've already shared too many things with you.'

* * *

June, and Appleby was busier than at any time of the year. To the rest of the country, June was a nice month, with the promise of summer and sunny days in the near future. To Appleby it was a bad month; a month of horse trading; of drunkenness; of brawls and the filth of gypsies, travellers and general ne'r-do-well traders. Since 1685 this ancient county town of the old county of Westmorland had hosted the main horse fair in the United Kingdom.

Gawpers came, to crowd the stone bridge across the river, and watch teenage rowdies ride bareback into the water, in order to wash their up-for-sale nags. The streets and kerbs were obstructed by vans and drays, and every thoroughfare was a course along which some young blood could gallop a horse for the benefit of some buyer.

Christmas Calvert moved through the throng. Occasionally he asked some gypsy a question. Sometimes he got an answer. At other other times all he got was a scowling reply. Nevertheless, when he returned to his car he had the information he needed, and was content.

*   *   *

Very pleasantly, Chris said, 'I didn't expect you to live. I was surprised—even shocked—when Avril told me.'

'Things go wrong.' The reply was in an equally pleasant tone.

From the wheelchair Pollard smiled across at Chris, who was relaxed on a rustic bench. They were in the grounds of a nursing home, not too far from Aberdeen. It was afternoon, the sun was strong enough to push its warmth into those who sought its rays, and the grass smelled sweet from a recent mowing.

Chris said, 'Will you walk again?'

'They tell me. With leg irons and elbow crutches.'

'Small mercies.'

'Just don't ask them from me, Calvert.'

'Would I?'

'You might be tempted.'

'A small temptation, I assure you.'

A group of starlings chattered, fluttered and fought on the grass of the lawn. Ill-tempered birds, forever squabbling. What they fought for was not apparent. Perhaps nothing. Perhaps it was merely the nature of their make-up.

The two men watched the furious starlings in

silence for a few moments. They sat alone, the bench alongside a tarmac path which diagonalled across the turf from the main building. The chair on the path, within easy listening distance.

Quietly—very seriously—Pollard said, 'I have every intention of killing you, Calvert.'

'I believe you ... that you'd *like* to.'

'Get me out of this damned chair. Get me upright. After that, watch your back.'

'It's why I came. Why I got this address. Why I want to explain certain fundamentals to you.'

Pollard waited, with narrowed eyes and flared nostrils.

Chris seemed to find something quite fascinating with the toe of one of his shoes, as he murmured, 'You have a daughter.'

'Leave Marie out of this, Calvert. It's between you and me. Kids aren't...'

'It's a game without rules, Pollard.' Chris continued to stare at the toe of his shoes. Then he raised his eyes and said, 'She's not where you think she is. She's not at the house of the minder, where D'Souza left her this morning. She hasn't been there since lunch.'

'She's my child. She's...'

'Of *course* she's your child. Why else would she have been removed from safe keeping?'

Pollard fought to control himself, then rasped, 'Where is she, Calvert?'

'I don't know. And...'

'One hair of her head. I swear. Touch one hair of her head, and you'll be screaming for mercy before I've finished with you.'

'I don't know where she is.' Chris's voice remained quite calm and under control. 'Just that she's safe. In good hands. And she'll remain safe, and in good hands while ever I live. If I die—other than in bed, and of old age—you can whistle goodbye to your daughter ... forever. Understood?'

'If you seriously think...'

'I *know*, Pollard. And when you've thought about it, you'll know. I remain safe and, as a bonus, Marie remains safe. That way you'll meet up with your daughter ... eventually. And, incidentally, don't dream up any plans for boiling oil, or splinters down the fingernails. I don't *know* where she is. What I don't know I can't tell you.'

Pollard stared deep hatred across the space between them. Chris smiled and stood up from the bench.

He said, 'That's it. That's why I came. To see you. To tell you. To explain a situation which just might interfere with your sweet dreams.'

He walked away, down the path and towards the gates of the nursing home.

Blackpool; late evening in November. The expression 'out of season' conveys nothing of the desolation. A place where, in June, July and August the barkers, the rock stalls, the pin-table arcades, the cafés, the ice cream parlours, the boozers, the night clubs, the strip joints, the fun palaces, the cheap-jack booths and the discos literally yell and fight for every last customer—every last sucker—seems to have died. Finished. 'In season' there are never less than half a dozen trams within sight and within earshot. The buses follow each other along the prom at twenty yard intervals, and less. But, 'out of season'! A bus occasionally. A tram every fifteen minutes, or thereabouts. It is as if the resort has exhausted itself and is fighting for a second wind, prior to the onslaught of one more punishing season. There never was a holiday resort more brash, more noisy, more straightforwardly vulgar, nor one that could give such an appearance of bleak unwantedness, once the crowds have gone home.

And on this November evening, as darkness slid insidiously into black night, the wind from the Irish Sea made a mockery of fur coats or wind-cheaters alike.

They stood in a tram shelter at Talbot

Square and, while their eyes smarted from the weather, they exchanged small-talk about a period long past.

Avril said, 'You took one hell of a risk, visiting him at the nursing home.'

'He was pinned to a wheelchair. I was away, before he could reach a telephone.'

'Ah yes, but...'

'And at a guess, the first job he did was to telephone whoever was supposed to be looking after the kid. To check I wasn't bluffing.'

'You weren't of course.'

'With Pollard?' Chris gave a quick, twisted smile. 'That would be like trying to pluck a tiger's whiskers. Oh, no. I'd made sure, before I met him in the grounds. His darling Marie was securely tied up in pink ribbon, and the only bargaining counter he'd ever take notice of. *And* she was for the big drop, if anything happened to me.' He paused, then added, 'And you, of course.'

'I didn't know that.'

'That's one of the reasons for you staying healthy.'

'It's a long time ago,' she mused.

'Yeah,' then, 'We've met up a few times, since.'

'Really?'

'Little jobs he's wanted doing.'

'Jobs?'

'Favours. Unimportant things he needed. He's asked me, and I've agreed.'

A solitary tram slowed and halted at the exit of the shelter. The automatic doors opened, and the conductor stepped to one side to give them easier access. Chris shook his head and made a backward movement of his body. The conductor looked slightly cross, closed the doors and rang the bell. The tram moved off on its way to Bispham.

Avril said, 'Let's find somewhere warmer than here ... shall we?'

'Yates's Wine Lodge.' Chris nodded at the neon sign above the entrance to a building, across Talbot Square. 'It's still there. Blackpool wouldn't be Blackpool without the wine lodge.'

'Why not? At least it's dry.'

1951

Some years back, it had been the talk of the district. How young Calvert had gone to war; had joined the RAF; had earned himself a commission and then, when the war ended, had returned to live in the same van, as an on-site gamekeeper. Not even head keeper, although the new head keeper left him strictly alone; orders, it was understood, from the young master—the new Sir Andrew Baxter, baronet. But the surprise had died down. Things had settled into a more-or-less pre-war perspective. The seasons continued to follow each other, as they had always done, and Chris reaffirmed his belief that the wild moors around Wharfedale, Old Cote Moor and Littondale were among the grandest places on God's earth.

It was one evening in April, when he approached the van from a full day's tramp along the valleys and rises, that he saw the Jowett Javelin parked by the van's door. It was a strange vehicle and Chris, suspicious as always, allowed the Savage to drop from the crook of his arm and curled his fingers around the trigger mechanism. He placed the brace of rabbits on a fallen log, just off the path.

He called, 'Hi, there! Do we have strangers in the van?'

Pollard said, 'Not strangers. Unexpected visitors. No more than that.'

Chris tightened his grip on the Savage, then realised that it was a much changed Pollard who stood in the doorway of the van. His legs were locked in leg-irons and he stood upright with the aid of elbow crutches. He was thinner—thin enough to be described as gaunt—and past suffering had darkened his eye sockets and lined his face.

Chris relaxed his grip on the rifle a little, walked warily towards the van and asked, 'Why the honour of the visit?'

'A job I'd like you to do.'

'Oh!'

'I'll pay ... but you're the only one I know capable of doing it.'

Chris said, 'Oh!' again and moved into the van's interior.

'The only one really capable,' repeated Pollard. He turned awkwardly on the irons and crutches and added, 'If you'll do it, of course.'

Chris sat on the edge of the bunk bed and waited.

In a quiet but steady voice, Pollard said, 'I'd like you to finish the job you started.'

'I'm sorry?' Chris frowned, not understanding.

'The Syrian,' said Pollard. 'This time, I want him dead.'

'You have a reason, of course.'

'A good enough reason.' Pollard's tone hardened. 'He married D'Souza. He's put her through hell for too long. It's time he vanished.'

'The old terminology,' said Chris softly.

'You can do it, Calvert.'

'*Anybody* can do it ... given a gun and enough strength to squeeze the trigger.'

'And get away with it, I mean.'

'Yeah ... but *will* I get away with it?'

'I'll see to that side of things.'

'Like last time?' mocked Chris.

'I mean it.' Pollard's voice was urgent. 'Twenty thousand pounds. Ten thousand up front and in your bank, before you even move. The rest when he's ready for burial.'

206

'So far,' said Chris in a mock-thoughtful voice, 'not a word about Marie D'Souza.'

'You know where she is.' The words bordered upon the dismissive.

'Not *where* she is. Just that she's safe and well.'

'That's good enough for now. Get this other thing finished first. Then you might trust me enough to take my word.'

'Don't place money on it, Pollard.'

'You'll see. This time I *need* you.'

*   *   *

From the steps of the caravan they watched the kids at play, chasing each other and rolling with the half-grown pups on the beachy surround of Blackwater Tarn. Jared Smith smoked some peculiar concoction of hedgerow herbs in a broken pipe and said, 'She loves to be free. Like a true Romany.'

Chris grunted, 'Except that she's *not*.'

'She could be,' insisted Jared. 'Morven loves her like her own.'

'A gypsy with flaxen hair,' observed Chris sardonically.

'Does it matter?'

They sat in silence for a few minutes, watching the two children and the dogs. Each with his own thoughts, and happy enough to be in the other's company.

In a quiet voice, Chris said, 'She should have

207

some schooling.'

In an equally quiet, but firm, voice Jared said, 'She learns. Each day, she learns a little more.'

'Reading and writing,' said Chris.

'Adding up and taking away?'

'That, too.'

'We manage well without.'

Morven joined them from the rear of the caravan. She saw them watching the children.

She said, 'She grows. A very healthy child.'

Jared said, 'He thinks she should have teaching.'

Morven's forehead puckered into a slight frown.

'Schooling,' explained Chris. 'I'd like her to be educated.'

'Not like us?' It was a challenging question. It could have led to open argument.

'*Different* to yours,' said Chris, gently.

Jared said, 'She knows how to trap and skin a rabbit.'

'And make it into a good stew,' added Morven.

'You've done well,' said Chris soothingly. 'You've *all* done well. You two, *and* the girl.'

'But not well enough,' said Morven unhappily.

'Morven. Jared.' Chris put feeling into his words. 'You've done marvels. More than I could have wished. She's a fine child, and you should be proud.'

'If we took her,' said Jared slowly. 'You'd never find us. Ever! Not even you.'

'You'd never sleep easily again,' promised Chris gently. 'You'd expect to see me round every corner.'

'We couldn't do that,' said Morven.

'I know.' Chris nodded.

Jared said, 'She can name every tree and bush in any wood—in any hedge. She knows the barks and the berries. What they're good for. What will harm her.'

'But now,' insisted Chris, 'she needs book learning.' He went on, 'You'll still be Uncle Jared and Aunty Morven. Just like I'll be Uncle Chris.'

Jared looked across at Morven. She looked miserable, but she nodded slowly, and Jared said, 'Your way, then.' He knocked the dottle from his pipe and said, 'But remember, now. She's only on loan. She's not *yours* ... any more than she's ours. Not even as *much* as she's ours,' he added.

* * *

'He comes from Barnsley,' said Pollard. 'Every Friday. Business at Barnsley, then onto the M1 at junctions thirty-seven or thirty-eight. Then he stops for a meal here, at Woolley Edge Service Area, before he tackles the London run.'

'A man of habit,' observed Chris.

'We all are.' Pollard's smile was cold and humourless. 'We eat at the same time. Often the same place. Sleep, bathe, shave, go for walks. Everything has its own rhythm. Everything, with everybody. We're all vulnerable . . if somebody takes the trouble to work out the rhythm.'

They were in the Service Area lorry park. They had a clear view of the entrance to the Granada Lodge Restaurant, and the car park in front of that entrance.

They were in a clapped-out furniture van and, at first sight, Chris had done nothing to hide his disgust.

'You're judging a book by its cover,' Pollard had said sourly. 'It has an engine and gears that can touch seventy in third, if necessary.'

'Will it be necessary?' Chris had asked.

'That's up to you . . . but it's there, if we need it.' Then, 'You've got the registered number firmly memorised?'

'Of course.'

'Not that it's too important. There aren't many pillar-box red Mercs on the road.'

'And you're going to drive?' Chris had glanced at the leg irons and crutches when he'd asked the question. He'd added, '*Can* you?'

'In this thing, as fast as *he* can in his Merc.'

'And?'

'Come round the back and examine the family furniture.'

Pollard had led the way to the rear of the

210

van; to where an open back showed stacked and lashed chairs, beds, mattresses, tables and sideboards. Chipped, scratched and broken, but all securely roped into position.

'There's a mattress in there,' Pollard had explained. 'It gives you a perfect prone shot, from under the junk and onto the road, behind the van. There's also a gun.'

'A gun? Why not...'

'Because,' Pollard had answered the question before it had been asked, 'guns leave their individual marks on bullets. Use *your* Savage and, in the unlikely event of anybody becoming suspicious the bullet can be traced to your gun. From you to me ... and, Calvert, that's not the way we do things. A "nobody's" gun. A Winchester, model 06 repeating rifle, with a dozen .22 long rounds in the magazine. With...'

'A toy gun,' Chris had snorted.

'A killer, with a .22 long round,' Pollard had contradicted.

'Maybe.'

'I want you to kill him ... not blow him to smithereens.'

'Fine.' Chris had shrugged. 'If you can keep the van steady.'

'Don't lose sleep. I can handle these controls as well as you can handle a gun.'

And it had been no less than the truth. The pedals—brake, accelerator and clutch—had all been adapted to Pollard's iron-stiff legs.

The seat, also, had been raised and tilted a little. From outside, the cab looked as broken down as the rest of the vehicle but inside it was a custom made-to-measure job.

And now they were watching the main entrance/exit to the Granada Lodge Restaurant at the Woolley Edge Service Area. Pollard was in the cab. Chris was standing at the cab door, smoking the last of a cigarette.

Suddenly Pollard said, 'That's him. Into the back. We have to beat him to the motorway.'

Chris heeled out what was left of the cigarette and, by the time he had swung himself into the rear of the van, Pollard had the engine ticking over and ready for the off.

They moved off, smoothly and without undue haste and settled into the southbound traffic of the motorway. Chris clambered over the ancient and scratched furniture, and settled himself on the waiting palliasse. He had a clear view of the road behind the van; an elongated view, from underneath a hand-wash-stand, with the Winchester held steady on top of a bed-box. It was a little like watching the following traffic through a large letter-box.

Chris worked the slide magazine and fed a round into the breech of the rifle. He moved his shoulders a little for extra comfort, and began to take deep breaths.

Pollard called through the glassless window leading from the cab, 'I've got him. He's overtaking. I'm moving into the fast lane. I'll edge into the overtaking lane, before he can pass.'

The following traffic seemed to move to the right as the van left the slow lane for the fast lane.

The red Merc was overtaking at speed. It was behind a speeding Jag. Pollard demonstrated his driving skill by smoothly pulling in behind the Jag, in the overtaking lane, and positioning the van immediately in front of the Merc.

It was a ridiculously easy shot. Not much more than ten yards. Shattering the windscreen and drilling a hole at the root of the Syrian's nose. He was dead before the Merc swayed out of control.

Pollard must have been watching through the driving mirror. As the windscreen shattered, he increased the speed of the van. Smoothly. Until he'd overtaken four or five cars and a lorry in the fast lane, then, into the fast lane.

Through his letter-box peep-hole Chris saw the Merc hit the central metal barriers, buck, stand on its rear wheels, then spin into the path of the southbound traffic and slam into the side of a bowser. Then Pollard moved into the fast lane and what must have been a multiple-car pile-up was hidden by the following vehicles.

The junction markers were coming up fast, and Pollard moved the van into the slow lane and left the motorway at junction thirty-eight.

It had been easy. Maybe too easy. North to Leeds. Then, skirting Bradford for Harrogate, and from there Ripon, Pateley Bridge and home.

By mid-afternoon, they were at the on-site keeper's van. Chris clambered from the back and assisted Pollard from the cab.

Pollard looked pleased.

He said, 'Did you hear it?'

'What?'

'On the local radio.'

'Was it mentioned?'

'A six-car shunt up.' The smile broadened a little. 'Two dead. Five in hospital. Congratulations, Calvert.'

'Worth the gun?' asked Chris. He added, 'As extra, I mean?'

'The cash, *and* the gun.' Pollard lost the smile and said, 'Why the gun?'

'I like guns, and this is a nice one.'

'Not long ago you called it a "toy".'

'I was wrong. At the right time and place it's a good gun.'

'Why not?' Pollard moved his shoulders. 'You fired it. The prints on it are yours ... so why not?'

'Thanks. And the cash?'

'The final cheque will be in the post tomorrow.' Then, 'Who knows, I might need you again.'

Pollard struggled his way back into the cab

214

and, as Chris opened the door to his van, the furniture van moved off.

1955

It had started life as a flash, country mansion, built by one of the wool barons. High living, fast women and Stock Exchange gambles had soon put a stop to that nonsense. Then the local authority had decided it was a very imposing structure in which to office its various officials. Nor had that been too good an idea, if only because the adjoining parkland—almost twenty acres of it—seemed ripe for any speculative builder eager to make a fast buck. No speculative builder had come along and so, in wild desperation this one-time-mansion-one-time-office-block had been sold, at a knock-down price, to a prize prat and his wife, to become a 'private' school for 'young ladies'... meaning the female offspring of parents who'd opted for overseas jobs, or parents who wanted rid of their family, in order that they might enjoy the occasional pleasures of parenthood, interrupted by the joyful freedom of multiple fornication.

In short, it was an expensive dumping ground for unwanted kids.

It required zero academic qualifications to become a pupil. Its teachers were as neat a mix of non-personalities and thick-headed

215

opinionates as it was possible to imagine. Useless pastimes like 'country dancing' and 'lino-block cutting' went great guns, but the more normal things—like the three Rs—were not counted as being too important. The miracle was that occasionally, one of the pupils managed to scrape into a university.

Nevertheless the school had 'grounds', including a kitchen garden, tennis courts, a leaf-blocked open air swimming pool, a coppice and enough mown grass to merit the name of 'cricket field'.

The 'cricket field' was in play this glorious July Sunday. The pupils were playing their annual fixture with the 'fathers' team'. Middle-management men, with the beginning of a personal executive gut had dolled themselves up in pads, gloves, flannels and an assortment of gaudy caps and were disporting themselves in a semi-serious game of bat-and-ball. It was meant to give pupils and staff, alike, the impression that the various daddies were great sports and only overgrown schoolboys at heart.

The pupils, on the other hand, were a mix of embarrassment, infuriation, boredom and determination to knock the stuffing out of these swaggering male ninnies.

Christmas Calvert was relaxing in a deck-chair, halfway round the field from the pavilion. He was watching the match through half-closed eyes and letting the sun smooth gentle warmth into his face. No other spectator was within twenty yards.

A voice from behind his back said, 'Mister Calvert?'

'Eh?' Chris tilted his head and opened his eyes.

'Mister Christmas Calvert?'

'And if I am?' Chris half-turned to give himself a better view of the stranger.

'They said you'd be here.'

' "They"?'

'From the hall. I went to your van, and you weren't there. I asked at the hall. They said you'd be here.'

'Okay. I'm here.' Chris hoisted himself higher in the deckchair.

'I was told,' said the stranger carefully, 'you might be the man I'm looking for.'

'Friend,' said Chris, 'you are being uncommonly coy.'

'It's necessary.'

'Why?'

'Because of what I'm about to ask.'

The stranger moved towards the front of the deckchair, and Chris had a good view of him for the first time. A middle-aged man, starting to go bald. Heavy moustache, full jowls and watery eyes. Despite the glorious weather he wore a dark blue suit, complete with waistcoat, a white shirt and a faintly patterned tie. He was a business man—one of the clowns who were cavorting around on the pitch.

217

'Why me?' asked Chris flatly. 'You don't know me. I don't know you, so why me?'

'You were—er—recommended.'

'Really.'

'By a man who said you could do it.'

'I see.'

'For a price, of course,' said the man hurriedly.

'Can we discuss what you're talking about?'

'Here?' The stranger looked startled.

'Why not? We're well beyond earshot of anybody else.' Chris made a movement with his hand. 'Sit down. On the grass—it's quite dry—and watch the game. And tell me about whoever it was who recommended me for this mysterious job you have in mind.' Then, 'It *is* some sort of a job, I take it.'

'Oh, yes.' The stranger lowered himself gingerly onto the grass alongside Chris's deckchair. He went on, 'A man we both know. He has difficulty walking.'

'Has he a name?'

'I suppose so. I don't know it, though. I met him at a party last Christmas. We both got drunk. Exchanged confidences.'

'That girl—that bowler.' Chris nodded towards the pitch. 'She bowls underarm, but she beats that prat with the bat, at least twice in every over.'

'But there's this other man. One of those ridiculously hearty people. Laughs all the time. No manners. No sense of decency...'

218

'She gives the ball a neat little tweak, just before it leaves her hand. Puts real spin on it. Pity she can't control it more...'

'... But my wife is besotted with him. I think they're having an affair. I'm sure of it. You can tell—y'know—you can *tell*...'

'... See that? She teases him out of his crease every time. If the damn wicket-keeper stood within reaching distance of the stumps, he'd be...'

'Damn it! I'm talking to you.'

Chris moved his attention from the pitch to the man sitting on the grass. He moved his head slowly. Deliberately.

He said, 'You think your wife is letting some other man cut the odd slice of cake, when you're not looking. You don't like it. Understandable. So-o ... hit him with something hard and heavy. Hit *her* with something hard and heavy.'

'I'm—I'm not that sort of man,' muttered the stranger.

'In that case, you deserve what you get.'

'I want him stopping,' ground the stranger.

'You want *me* to hit him with something hard and heavy?'

'I want you to *kill* him.'

'As bad as that?' Chris raised his eyebrows.

'The man—the man who suggested that I see you—said you'd do it. For ten thousand.'

'Ten thousand?' mused Chris gently. 'That's a lot of money.'

'I want my wife back.'

'*You* kill him,' teased Chris.

'I—I—I daren't. I might make a mess of it.'

'Murder, my friend, is a messy process.'

'Please!' pleaded the stranger. 'Please help me.'

Sweat was running in tiny rivulets down his cheeks. His face was ugly with misery and he wasn't too far from tears.

In a curiously gentle, sombre voice Chris said, 'Some details. Eh? First of all, who are you? Where do you live?'

The stranger fingered a visiting card from the top pocket of his jacket. 'That's my firm. Home address at the bottom.'

Chris read the card and murmured, 'Anthony Willis. And you make gaskets.'

'A small firm.' The stranger swallowed, then added, 'Ten thousand. That's all I can afford. Honestly.'

Chris nodded, as if satisfied.

'Tell me—y'know—how do I get it to you?' Willis was almost eager. 'A cheque? Cash, maybe?'

'Cash,' said Chris.

'How?'

'Small denomination notes. Nothing bigger than twenty.'

'Oh!'

'It will fit into a brief-case. Take my word. It's not so much.'

'It—it seems a lot. That's all.'

220

'If you're going to start haggling, take a walk,' said Chris coldly. 'You sought me. I didn't seek you.'

'No! I'm sorry. I didn't mean it that way.' Willis's face sweated even more. 'Of course you'll do it. Of course I'll pay. Just that— y'know—it isn't a thing you do every day. Is it?'

'I might,' said Chris quietly. Then, 'I need a photograph of your wife. A good one.'

'Of course.' Willis fumbled a wallet from his inside pocket and took out a colour photograph. He said, 'That's her. A good likeness. And I've written the number of his car on the back.'

*   *   *

Pollard looked annoyed. He'd answered the front door bell, and his eyes had widened when he'd seen Chris standing on the doorstep of the flat.

It was a ground floor flat in what had once been a nursing home. A solid, grey building, standing in its own laurel-heavy grounds. In a town with more than its fair share of nursing homes, this had been a Victorian gem, but medicine and nursing had progressed, and the thick stone walls had not lent themselves to easy adaptation. Instead ... flats. In the better part of a very snooty town, and within easy walking distance of the shopping centre.

221

Pollard said, 'How the hell did you...'

'You sent a man to me,' interrupted Chris.

'Eh?'

'He wants a rather nasty job done to his wife's boyfriend.'

'Oh!'

'Last Christmas, you said I might help him. At a party. You were both drunk. He knows where the party was held ... and *they* know your address. It's all done by mirrors.'

'You'd better come inside.' Pollard stood to one side, and Chris entered the flat.

The impression was of high-ceilinged rooms and wide, high window spaces; of absolute privacy and an absence of outside-world noise.

Pollard waved Chris to a deep, comfortable armchair, then asked, 'Well?'

'I've accepted the invitation ... more or less.'

'Good.'

'What rake-off do you get?'

'Nothing. I shall be doing nothing. Whatever he pays, it's all yours.'

'No.' Chris shook his head. 'I need a cut-out point.'

'Sensible.'

'You.'

'I can't see how...'

'I'll send you a key, by post. Leeds City Station. Lock-up property. Use the key, bring the contents of the left-luggage box here. I'll collect it later.'

'Leeds Station?'

'A busy place. Dodge around a bit if you get suspicious.'

'If I get suspicious,' said Pollard, 'I shall come straight back here.'

'Understood.' Chris nodded. Then, 'Will you be using the same van as last time?'

'Good God, no. I have an adapted Austin.'

'Fine.' Chris smiled. 'Ten per cent? A round thousand, for your trouble?'

'It sounds fair.'

'It should buy you a fish and chip supper.'

'Fish and chips? Here, in Harrogate?' Pollard's smile had little humour in it. 'You've lived in the backwoods too long, Calvert.'

*　　*　　*

'It is,' said the headmistress, 'rather unusual. Part-way through a term. The child may suffer no small disadvantage.'

'I would consider it a great favour,' said Chris politely. 'I should expect to pay the full term's fee, of course. But the school she's in at the moment has turned out to be most unsatisfactory.'

They were in the headmistress's study. A large room, lined on three walls with glass-fronted bookshelves. With a display cabinet showing cups, shields and platters won at various sports. The high window looked across two miles of moorland to the waters of Bridlington Bay.

223

The light shimmered on the distant waves and a tiny blip on the horizon might have been a passing vessel.

The headmistress pondered on the problem for a few moments, then said, 'I presume you wish to change schools as soon as possible.'

'Starting here next Monday, if possible.'

'Good heavens!'

'It will *be* possible, I hope.'

'I—er—I suppose so. There is, of course, the business of the uniform, and all the other things she'll need. We like them to have their own hockey stick. Their gym outfit. Shoes. A large tuck box for the foot of their bed. Uniformity, you see. We count that as very important. Then no girl feels under-privileged.'

'There'll be a shop,' said Chris. 'There always is. Some shop specialising in the outfit required by this school.'

'Oh, yes. Scarborough. There's a slightly less expensive shop at Bridlington, but if you use the Scarborough shop they know exactly what we want, and they have a large stock.'

'That's it, then.' Chris stood up. 'Thank you for your time, headmistress. You've been most kind. I'll be here with Marie at nine o'clock, Monday morning.'

*   *   *

The Anthony Willis Gasket Company was a

tiny, back-street business, with an office not much larger than a Portakabin. Willis looked very uncomfortable and kept glancing through the office window, to where various manually operated pieces of machinery pressed and moulded gaskets.

He almost moaned, 'You shouldn't have come here.'

'I'm buying gaskets,' said Chris flatly.

'They'll—they'll ... Somebody will recognise you.'

'You needed to be seen.' Then, 'Get it done with. Answer a few questions, then I'll be on my way.'

'What sort of questions?'

'When is it your night out?'

'Eh?'

'Your night out with the boys. When do you ...'

'I don't. I'm—er—I'm a member of the local Rotary. They meet every alternative Thursday. But I rarely go. Since my wife ...'

'That's when lover boy called?' said Chris expressionlessly.

'I think so.'

'Start going again. Get enthusiastic.'

'It's not as easy as ...'

'Start "rotating" Willis. Give yourself a break. Make yourself an alibi.'

'Oh!'

'Let me tell you something, friend.' Chris leaned forward in his chair. 'A wife gets

225

murdered ... suspect number one is hubby. Always! A wife's boyfriend gets murdered. Again, hubby is the first name in the frame. It follows. So-o, he'd better have some pretty hot proof that he was somewhere else when the boyfriend's heart stopped functioning. He'd better *be* somewhere else. He'd better have witnesses. And he'd better know Sweet F.A. about the "how", the "why" and the "who". Get that clear in your mind.'

'I—I wouldn't,' stammered Willis. 'I wouldn't *ever*...'

'That's *my* problem,' said Chris coldly. 'Any suggestion that you even *might* start singing arias ... and you follow the boyfriend. Savvy?'

'I...' Willis nodded wildly. 'Of course. That's—that's understood.'

*　　*　　*

The railway wagon that had once housed Daisy, the donkey, was now an open-doored workshop. Makeshift, perhaps, but sufficient for what Chris wanted. There was a workbench, various files and rasps, hammers, chisels, screwdrivers ... enough tools to perform Do-It-Yourself repairs upon various firearms Chris had amassed.

There was a small, but serviceable vice, bolted to a small, but solid bench, and, in the jaws of this vice, held firmly between folds of cloth, to prevent accidental misshaping, was a

.22 long round of ammunition. Chris was working on the nose of the bullet, with a small, watchmaker's file.

He was creating an illegality. A dum-dum bullet. In effect an explosive bullet, which would explode on impact, because of the compression of air in its nose since it left the barrel of the gun.

That fanciful collection of international absurdities known as 'The Rules of War' had long since outlawed dum-dum bullets. They were, it was argued, too 'inhuman'. They rarely wounded. They almost invariably killed.

Officially, no ammunition firm manufactured dum-dums. Unofficially they could be obtained, via under-the-counter fiddles. And, of course, they could be made; an ordinary round of ammunition could be turned into a dum-dum in a matter of minutes.

Chris was making dum-dum bullets.

*   *   *

He waited for the evenings to grow darker; for the days to become shorter. He wanted dusk—that half-and-half period, between daylight and darkness—when the eyes of both pedestrians and motorists have not yet become accustomed to the absence of light. A difficult period in which to see, unless dark glasses have been worn and night vision has been deliberately created.

227

For weeks he'd watched Willis leave home for the Rotary get-together. Each alternate Thursday the worried, frightened little man had left the house and driven off towards the town centre. Twice, he'd followed Willis. To the three-star hotel where the local Rotary members held their meetings.

He'd watched lover-man arrive at the home after Willis had departed. Watched the wife greet him at the door; the door close and, shortly afterwards, the light go on in the front bedroom. It was a classic case of cuckolding. A simple blow-his brains-out situation.

And now, he was crouched behind the shelter of a privet hedge, in the garden of a house opposite Willis's home. The house was unoccupied; the 'For Sale' sign emphasised this important fact. It was unoccupied, and it was showing the first signs of neglect. The hedge was untrimmed. The grass of the lawn needed mowing. The whole place *looked* unoccupied.

The street lighting was starting to come on. Tall, goosenecked standards, with yellow lights that seemed to intensify the shadows rather than combat the darkness. It was drizzling slightly. A steady, soaking downpour that kept pedestrians indoors and ensured that drivers concentrated upon the mirrored road ahead. A perfect night for a killing.

The Winchester .22 rifle was leaning against the hedge. It was going to be a kneeling shot,

228

with a slightly upward trajectory. Not a difficult shot if he took care. He began to draw deep breaths of oxygen into his lungs. A trick; a means of ensuring that his hands and arms remained steady when the moment came.

He crouched there. Waiting. Not impatient. Not unduly worried. Nothing. He would have expressed surprise had somebody suggested that he might feel some sort of emotion.

The Volvo braked to a halt, and Chris dropped to one knee and reached for the Winchester. The foresight and the V of the backsight had been touched with tiny spots of fluorescent paint. He rested the barrel in the fork of an already-chosen branch of the privet and carefully lined up the sights.

The man left the Volvo and crossed the pavement. He climbed the shallow steps and pressed the bell-push.

Behind, and slightly below, the left ear. It would—*should*—turn his brain to mush. Twenty-yards? No more than that. A ridiculously easy shot.

The hall light was switched on. There was a pause, then the door opened and, as the door opened, Chris squeezed the trigger.

Outside it was wet and cold. Inside it was hot and stuffy, with a thickening fug of tobacco smoke. They sat at a corner table away from the bulk of customers. She sipped at a rum-and-peppermint. He drank at a whisky-and-soda. Neither of them seemed to be enjoying the minor drinking session.

She smiled and murmured, 'I never figured you as a cheapskate.'

'Cheap?' He looked puzzled.

'Ten thousand for a killing.'

'It's all he had. Anyway ... *nine* thousand. Pollard took his cut.'

'Cheap,' she repeated.

'For one trigger squeeze?'

She said, 'Chris, you don't kill people in this country and simply get away with it.'

'Don't you?' Now he smiled and tasted his drink.

'*Do* you?' She looked surprised. Maybe shocked.

'A guy called Browne,' he said gently. 'That wasn't his real name, of course. But I called him Browne, and he called me Greene ... always with an "e" at the end.' He paused, then went on. 'I was getting a little strapped. And why not? The gratuity from the RAF had been generous enough, and money *meant* something in those days. But Marie's new school had to be paid for, and it wasn't cheap.

'That was when Jared and Morven arrived. Less than a week into the New Year.'

1956

Chris saw the caravan across the dark water of the tarn. In its usual spot; in the shelter of the copse, with the horse tethered out of the worst of the weather. Despite the dogs and the teenage son moving around the camp, it looked strangely quiet. Neither Jared nor Morven were in sight. Chris hoisted the twelve-bore Venere into a more comfortable position under his arm and set off, across the frost-rimmed turf for the caravan.

It was cold—it was January—but the real iron fist of winter had yet to come. The tarn was not yet frozen over. The tiny wild creatures that spend their winter in whatever shelter they can find had not yet gone to ground.

The boy saw Chris from a distance. He moved to the caravan, and Morven came down the steps and started walking to meet him. The boy ran off in the opposite direction, towards the broken-down boathouse which nobody ever used.

Morven turned and walked alongside him.

She said, 'Jared's dying, sir.' It was a sombre

statement, and made absolute conviction.

'Is that what a doctor says?'

'He won't see a doctor.'

'If he's ill...'

'He's dying, sir. We know these things. His lungs. They don't work any more.'

'It's maybe the cold. If we get him into a warm place...'

'Listen!' She stopped and touched his arm. He too stopped and, in the stillness, he heard the rattle and rasp of a man fighting for enough breath to keep alive. 'For weeks now,' she said. 'It's got worse. The boy traps a little. I get roots. For broth and poultices.'

'He has to see a doctor,' insisted Chris.

'He's still master, and he says "No".'

'For God's sake, Morven...'

'*He's* master,' she said tightly. 'He's been a good man. I won't refuse him now.'

Together they hurried to the caravan.

In the built-in bed at the far end of the van, an obviously dying Jared watched them with burning eyes. He hauled breath into his lungs, like a weary man dragging at an impossible weight. He exhaled in a noisy rush.

'Jared!' Chris climbed into the van and bent over the sick man. 'You need medicine, Jared. You should be in hospital.'

'No.' Jared Smith's stare was almost hypnotic in its fierce intensity. He croaked, 'No doctor. No hospital. The boy knows what to do,' then he fell back, exhausted by the effort

232

of speaking.

Morven said, 'Can you carry him outside, sir?'

'Outside?'

'It's what he wants. We've discussed it, sir. He has to be helped outside.'

There was no arguing with such determination, and Chris bent, lifted the thin form of his friend, and carefully carried him down the caravan steps.

The boy had hauled an ancient rowing boat to the shallows and he jumped into the water, waded ashore, then helped Chris to carry the sick man to the boat, and prop him against the bulwark. Chris remained silent. His movements had a dream-like quality, as he allowed the boy to dictate each move. He stood there holding the boat steady, while the boy returned to the caravan, then re-joined him, carrying the Venere and a strong, canvas sack, held closed with builders' ropes. He tossed the sack and the gun into the boat, then held it steady while Chris climbed aboard.

The boy joined Chris and Jared, then lifted oars from the bottom of the boat and began to row.

Almost a hundred yards from the shore the boy stopped rowing. He leaned forward and fastened the sack to his father's legs, just below the knee. The contents of the sack were heavy and the boy had difficulty in heaving it into place.

233

'Lead,' he gasped as an explanation. 'Collected, but not stolen. Old lead, from builders' yards.'

Chris nodded, but didn't yet understand.

He understood when, with an obvious effort, Jared lifted the shotgun and wrapped his lips around the double snout of the twin barrels.

'Please,' whispered the boy. 'It's what he's been waiting for.'

'I—I . . .' Chris found his mouth was too dry for any coherent speech.

Carefully—gently—the boy lifted the Venere and guided the stock into Chris's unwilling hands. Jared held the twin barrels in both hands and kept his lips wrapped around the muzzles.

'Please!' pleaded the boy, and Jared gave a tiny, silent nod of agreement.

Chris settled the stock against the thick flesh of his thigh. He thumbed both hammers back, then curled fingers around the two triggers; forefinger around the front trigger, second finger around the rear trigger. He glanced at Jared a last time. Something like a smile touched the dying man's eyes and he gave a second, tiny nod.

Chris tightened his fingers. The gun kicked against the muscle of his thigh. The double shot echoed around the basin of the tarn. Jared's body seemed to leap a few inches into the air, then fell backwards into the water, and was held by his knees catching on the upper edge of the bulwark, and the lead-filled sack being caught beneath one of the seats. The boy gave a strangled sob, threw himself forward and dragged the sack free. There was a slight flurry, the boat rocked, then steadied itself ... and Jared Smith was gone. He had never been. He hadn't existed. He was no more than a few bursting bubbles rising to the surface of the tarn.

The boy hauled for shore. Chris forced himself to look at the boy's face, and saw misery the like of which he neither knew nor comprehended. The tears ran in tiny rivers down both cheeks. The sobs seemed to threaten to choke.

'It's—er—it's what he wanted,' said Chris gruffly.

The boy tried to nod but, unaccountably, seemed unable to move his head.

*   *   *

Thirty minutes later Chris was back at his own van, and meeting the man he came to know as 'Browne'.

The car—an expensive but, nevertheless, very nondescript car—was parked on the turf in front of the van entrance. The driver—like the car, very expensive, but equally nondescript—was relaxed in the driver's seat, with the window wound down.

He smiled and said, 'Any luck?'

'Eh?'

'I heard the shooting. Did you bag anything?'

'Crows,' grunted Chris. 'Vermin ... that's all.'

'Good.' The man opened the door and climbed from the car. He wore a well-cut, dark grey suit, black shoes, white shirt and club tie. He was hatless, and sported a neatly trimmed military moustache. His hair was a touch too long, and brushed into careful wings above his ears. His voice was a neat cross between the clipped speech of an officer in some popular regiment, and a public school drawl. He held out his hand and said, 'Calvert, I presume.'

'Yes.'

'Browne.' As they shook hands he added, 'Delighted to meet you, Calvert. I've heard a lot.'

'About *me*?'

'Something of a legend, old boy.'

'I don't see why.'

'A mutual friend. Thinks the world of you.'

'Pollard?' growled Chris. 'Has *he* ...'

'Uncle Claude,' said Browne. 'Highly recommended by Uncle Claude.' Then, as Chris looked puzzled, 'Claude Dansey, old chap. You worked for him during the war.'

'Oh!' Chris nodded. 'As you say ... I worked for him. Some sort of an undercover outfit ...'

'He still runs them.' Browne chuckled

quietly. 'He's busier than ever. He's quite sure you could help.'

Browne waved a slightly languid hand in the direction of the van's door, and said, 'Shall we ...?'

'Oh, yes. Come inside, I'll put a brew on, and you can tell me what you want.'

Thirty minutes later they were settled in chairs. The stove was pumping out heat. They were sipping hot tea, laced with brandy from a hip-flask produced by Browne, and that gentleman was delivering a speech which—or so it seemed—he had either rehearsed, or delivered more than once in the past.

He said, 'After June sixth, 1944—indeed, after September third, 1943, when Italy was invaded—after D-Day, in fact, the whole of Europe was awash with uniforms. Combatants were killed. They deserted. They died in hospital. They escaped from PoW camps. In late August, 1944—indeed *from* that date, until years after hostilities ceased—small fortunes were made in Paris via the sale of spare uniforms. And more than uniforms. Identity cards. Dogtags. Everything. Down to underclothes and socks. Watches. Shoes and boots. The genuine article, you understand. Not faked. Not counterfeit. The real thing. It's hard to believe, but it's a fact. Given enough money it was possible to get rigged out as a three-star general in the United States Army ... and, moreover, prove that that's who you

237

were. Similarly with the French forces. The Belgian forces. The Polish forces. The English forces.

'There was a non-stop shuttle service between the French and Belgian ports and the south coast of England. Air lifts every day. Between Europe and America. Men used to thumb lifts—and *get* lifts—and no questions asked.'

He paused, sipped his tea, then continued, 'At the same time, there was a great rush for anonymity by what we might call the "middle management" of the SS. And the Gestapo, of course. We collared most of the top boys before they could get away—but thousands of the hounds who did the dirty work, and enjoyed doing the dirty work, ran for it.

'A lot made for America. Then down, through Mexico and Costa Rica and into South America. Brazil. Bolivia. Argentina. Quite a large ex-Nazi community built up. Indeed, at one time it was seriously thought that the *Fourth* Reich might be founded in that area. They still need to be watched. Rumours still abound. There's *still* the possibility that Hitler's deputy, Martin Borman, is holed up there ... but that's the problem of the USA authorities. We have enough on with the United Kingdom.'

Another pause. Another sip at the brandy-laced tea. Then, 'Language was no problem, of course. Thanks to far too many exchange student schemes before the war, lots of the class we're talking about could speak perfect English. They fitted in. They vanished. They're still around. Every community ... spattered with a few one-time Hitler fan club members.' He chuckled quietly. 'Eventually they'll become completely Anglicised. Their pure, racial hogwash will be diluted into a typical British acceptance of ordinariness.'

'In that case...' began Chris.

'But not so the Communists,' interrupted Browne. 'They're not running away *from*. They're deliberately coming *into*.

'Stalin and his KGB goons saw the opportunity and grasped it. An open door. They too can speak English. They too can pass muster. The invitation was too good to refuse. God only knows how many arrived, before somebody realised the mistake. Only that they're in here. They're nibbling away at the lower classes. At the British Labour Party. At local government. At the trade union structure. At everything.' A quick frown came and went. 'They were never allies, you know, old man. Co-belligerents. That's what Churchill called them. We had a common enemy, but we were never friends.

'And now—when we've almost strangled the cross-channel trips they're coming in at fishing ports in the Highlands and Islands. Not much check. A Russian boat pulls in to unload—to fuel up—anything. A group of maybe half a dozen go ashore for a drink. It's anybody's guess whether half a dozen—or even the *same* half dozen—return to the ship. It's as easy as taking pennies from a blind man. Enemies of the Realm, old chap. That's the official name for them. As dangerous as the Nazi crowd. Deadly. And they have to be eliminated.'

Browne stopped, and seemed to wait for some sort of reaction.

Chris moistened his lips, then said, 'That's why you're here?'

'That's why.' Browne nodded.

'Dansey taught us to kill,' mused Chris.

Again, Browne nodded.

'And *that's* why you're here.'

Browne placed an almost empty cup on the nearby table and said, 'You'd be classified as a civil servant.'

'A government killer.'

'You'd be paid a retainer of a thousand pounds a month...'

'There shouldn't *be* such people. Not in peacetime.'

'... to be paid into the Fleet Street branch of Coutts, on the first of every month...'

'If I'm caught, I'll be thrown to the dogs. I know people like Dansey well enough to know *that*.'

'... This month's retainer has already been paid...'

'I'd be a fool. I'd be *mad*.'

'... There's a bonus for each job. Usually ten

thousand. Sometimes a little more. Sometimes a little less. Paid into the same bank. Impossible to trace. One hundred per cent safe. And nobody—*nobody!*—will ever be able to connect you with any of the work you carry out for us. You'll remain an on-site gamekeeper. Sir Andrew has already been approached. The job's yours—the gamekeeping job, I mean—while ever you want it. That's all he knows, and he won't ask questions.'

Browne took a sealed envelope from his inside pocket, and placed it on the table alongside the cup.

He said, 'The details of your account at Coutts. I suggest you open an account at the local Nat West. They'll transfer the money from London whenever it's paid in. Again ... no questions asked.'

Chris stared across at Browne's face, but could determine no emotion. Pleasant good manners. No more than that, but that in abundance.

Browne continued, 'The problem of Marie's school fees would be solved. I don't have to tell you that. A lot of your troubles would disappear overnight.'

'And so,' said Avril musingly, 'you became one of the people who aren't there.' She stared at the road ahead, as the Volvo spewed the motorway out behind them. 'One of the creatures of legend. A character who only exists in lurid crime novels. The government killer. The "official" assassin ... but of course, they don't exist. Do they?'

'I wish they didn't,' muttered Chris, and there was a deep sadness in the words.

They were on the M55, travelling towards the junction with the M6, then north to the Forton Service Area, and a civilised snack at an uncivilised hour. Yates's Wine Lodge had wearied them; the fug and the faint stench of stale booze had done nothing to ease the mounting feeling of a wasted day. They'd caught a taxi to the South Shore car park and had picked up Avril's Volvo and were now speeding towards warmth and food. The motorway was quiet enough; the hour, the time of the year and the weather all tended to dissuade all except essential travellers from venturing out.

Chris sat hunched in the front passenger's seat. Miserable with his private thoughts. Wondering why the hell they were there, and why this apparently unnecessary meeting had

had to take place.

He muttered, 'A stupid life. A wasted life.'

'Eh?' Avril gave a quick glance, sideways, at her passenger. She said, 'Whose?'

'Mine.'

'And now you're pitying yourself. That's not like the old Chris. Whatever else, he didn't waste too much time on self-pity.'

'The "old" Chris,' echoed Chris bitterly. 'You never knew him except during the war years. In those days he was crazy. We all were. The whole world ... utterly crazy. But gradually...'

He left the sentence unfinished.

'We grew up,' she suggested. 'We learned more sense.'

'Something like that. Certainly we lost a lot of the joy.'

'I wonder,' she mused, 'whether all elderly people think like that. Are so damned miserable. Are so sure they've been short-changed.'

'Everybody has their moments,' said Chris and the smile was a little twisted but, nevertheless, genuine.

'Everybody,' she agreed.

'It's just that, sometimes, they get smothered under all the bad memories.'

Browne had left. Without opening it, Chris had stashed the sealed envelope in the pages of one of the books from his fairly large library. He'd swilled the teacups. He'd read a couple of articles in one of the country magazines and, as the afternoon daylight darkened into an early dusk, he'd performed his ablutions, undressed and climbed into the bunk bed. The light from a pressure lamp gave ample illumination to continue reading, and the warmth from the stove kept the hardening frost at bay.

The tap on the van door made him sit more upright and reach a hand towards the nearby Savage.

He called, 'Who is it?'

'Morven. It's Morven Smith, sir. May I come in?'

'Of course.'

She opened the door and for a moment—before she closed the door behind her—the frost reached into the van with icy fingers.

She stood motionless in the lamplight and, for perhaps the first time, Chris recognised her as an uncommonly handsome woman. Not beautiful. Not pretty. But handsome and complete, with dark hair touched with grey and a figure that was both full and held well.

She said, 'I bathed, sir. And rubbed myself

with sweet-smelling herbs.'

Her hands went to the back of the wide-skirted dress, she gave a quick shrug of the shoulders, and she stood, without movement and without shame, as naked as the day of her birth. The pubic hair matched the hair on her head, and was thick and dark, but in no way unseemly. Her back was straight, and her breasts full, and proudly held. She moved towards the bed, and her motion was like that of a deer; not a fawn, but a fully grown deer—a mature and haughty hind—ready to accept and satisfy any arrogant stag ready to mount her.

As she folded the bedclothes back, she whispered, 'Chris, sir, you were Jared's friend. His great friend. Your last service to him was to give him peace. There must be a reward, Chris, sir. My man would demand it, if he could. I will give you a night to remember on the day you die. My reward, for your kindness to Jared.'

She climbed onto the bed and straddled him. The jungle of pubic hair rubbed against his belly and an already magnificent erection throbbed and quivered in carnal anticipation.

*   *   *

Spring came early that year. The white of winter gave way to the golds and greens of the new season. Wildlife gradually awakened. Lambs were born in makeshift shelters on the fells. The hedgehogs crawled from their winter nests and the little creatures scurried around, as if eager to make up a great slice of lost time.

Willis visited the van one fine evening, as Chris was sitting on the step cleaning and oiling the Venere. The car pulled up on the turf of the tiny clearing, and Willis climbed out.

Chris nodded a not-too-friendly welcome.

Willis stood in front of him, looked down and blurted, 'I'm going to the police. I thought it only fair to tell you.'

'The police?' Chris pretended not to understand, and leaned the shotgun against the van side.

'My wife.' Willis wasn't far from breaking point. His voice trembled with a weight of emotion he could hardly control. 'Do you—do you know what you did to her?'

'I killed her fancy man. It's what you paid me to do.'

'You—you made his head explode in her face. *Explode* in her face.'

'Dum-dums do that sometimes,' said Chris flatly.

'She passed out.'

'Really? I didn't wait to see.'

'She was under sedation for almost two weeks.'

'It's what you wanted.'

'No! Never!'

'Grow up, Willis. It's what you *wanted*.'

'She blames me.'

246

'She's a good guesser.' Chris almost smiled.

'Christ, man, you've destroyed her sanity. She's unstable with it.'

'A fair question.' Chris stood up slowly as he spoke. 'Are you stupid enough to believe that running to the police might bring back her sanity?'

'It might help. It will help *me*.'

'And me?'

'I'm giving you the chance, Calvert. That's why I'm here. I want to give you the chance to run.'

'Let's talk it over.' Chris turned his back on the distraught man and entered the van.

'It won't do any good.' Willis followed him into the gloom of the van, and kept talking. 'I've had enough. I can't take any more. Whatever you say, I won't...'

Chris had reached the table. He'd quietly opened one of the end drawers, and now the Luger was in his hand, its snout pointing at the man whose wife he'd driven mad.

'I'm not saying *anything*,' said Chris, quietly. 'You've made a decision. And, if you recall, I made a promise. What I'd do if you ever made that decision.'

'No! You can't!'

'You're a weak man, Willis,' purred Chris. 'You're also a fool, and I've no intention of being part of your foolishness.'

Willis held his arm out, hands palm forward, as if to ward off the Luger's bullets. He turned

247

and stumbled down the van steps, then ran, drunkenly, for the parked car.

Chris stepped to the van door, raised the pistol in a two-handed grip and squeezed off three quick shots. The first hit Willis in the shoulder, the second and third smashed into his spine. He lay on the ground about three yards from the car, twitching and making weak, moaning sounds. Chris descended the steps, moved a little nearer, then finished the job off with a round through the head.

*   *   *

Chris knew Buttertubs Pass by this time. Since Seth Calvert had first taken him there, he'd visited this, the high pass between Wensleydale and Swaledale, on numerous occasions. For a quick change of scenery. To remind himself of the basic wildness of open, Yorkshire moorland. Wilder, even, than his own gamekeeper's beat. Wilder, in his opinion, than any countryside in the United Kingdom.

And the deep—some claimed bottomless—limestone shafts from which the pass got its name still fascinated him. You want rid of somebody, or something? You want that person—that thing—never to be seen again? Drop them, or it, into a convenient buttertub ... then forget all about it.

He left Buttertubs Pass without Willis's body and drove Willis's car down the slope and

248

along the Nidd Valley until he reached the outskirts of Knaresborough. He parked on a lay-by, up a side road, and waited for dawn. When he wasn't cat-napping he was listening to the early morning birdsong; the tits, the finches, the wagtails. He could identify each call; the trill of the blackbird, the quick pipping of the thrush, the various mimicry of the starlings.

The sky in the east lightened a little, and he left the car. When the road was clear, he raised the bonnet and loosened the petrol inlet to the pump. He closed the bonnet, then took the cap from the petrol tank. He lifted the boot and took out the two-gallon jerry can he'd brought from the van. He opened the car doors—first the front door, then the rear door—and splashed petrol on the upholstery. He emptied what was left of the petrol onto the floor of the car and ran a short trail of it to a nearby gap in the hedge.

He checked that the road was clear, went to the gap, climbed through, then tossed a lighted match onto the petrol. He was away before the flame reached the car; was a field-length away before the body of the car flared up; was almost two field-lengths away before the tank exploded in a great spout of fire.

He stood at a bus stop, across country from the lay-by. The glow showed on the sky-line, behind his back. The bus arrived and as he climbed aboard he asked, 'What is that—a stack fire?'

'Could be.'

'Spontaneous combustion,' he suggested.

'I wouldn't be surprised.' The conductress showed complete non-interest.

He rode the bus to Knaresborough, changed to another bus for Harrogate, then caught a train to Pately Bridge.

When he arrived back at the van, he climbed into bed to catch up on lost sleep.

*　　*　　*

His first 'official business' took place three months later. It was mid-August, with a deep blue sky and tiny powder-puff clouds floating gently from horizon to horizon. The instructions came in a letter. They would have meant nothing, had the letter been mistakenly opened. A first-class return rail ticket from Pately Bridge to Mablethorpe, a page torn from a railway timetable, with a route underlined in red and the torn-off corner of a playing card showing the seven of spades.

On the seventh of that month he caught the train to Mablethorpe.

The journey brought back memories. Vacated and weed-strewn runways. Empty, broken-down hangars. Airfields already being taken over by grass. It saddened him a little; forced him to look back—glance over his shoulder—weigh the good times against the bad. The assessment did little to lighten his mood.

Browne was waiting for him at the station. He introduced him to the stocky, dark-haired Welshman.

'Greene, this is White. You'll be working together occasionally.'

They shook hands, and the Welshman grinned mischievously. The name 'White' was in no way appropriate.

They left the station and climbed into the back of a Morris van. Bench seats were along the sides of the van, and Browne faced them and briefed them, as they rode away from the coast.

He said, 'Something new. We're throwing a scare into one of the opposition. With luck, he'll be able to undo some of the damage.' The brief smile came and went; a mere grimace, without humour. 'They don't scare easily. The trouble-makers are gearing themselves up to put the kybosh on Calder Hall nuclear power station, when it comes on stream later this year. The Queen's scheduled to open it in October. *They* are determined to do all they can to upset the apple cart. They have to be stopped ... obviously.' He paused, then went on, 'Fortunately there's a small core of "organisers". You'll meet two today. We're going to throw one back into the nest, hope he has nightmares and warn him what might happen if he doesn't, personally, smooth out

251

the kinks. It's a new venture on our part. Let's hope, for everybody's sake, that it comes off.'

'A few bones broken. Eh?' White's voice was almost eager. The Welsh lilt seemed to give the words an extra, cheerful menace.

'Nothing so crude,' drawled Browne.

Little more was said until, slightly more than half an hour later, the van braked to a halt. They climbed out, and as far as the eye could see was open grassland, criss-crossed with strips of concrete. They were alongside a slightly broken-down Nissen hut, and as he led the way into the hut Browne delivered further instructions.

'Boiler suits, over flying jackets. It's going to be chilly.' Then as he saw Chris looking at the view, he added, 'A wartime Yankee airfield. Fortresses used to take off from here.' He smiled. 'The local ladies miss their American candy bars, I'm told.'

Chris grunted, then followed the other two into the Nissen hut.

They struggled into flying gear, then pulled over-sized boiler suits over the lot. They were awkward and sweating by the time they'd geared themselves up, but Browne reassured them.

'We won't be *quite* in the slip-stream ... but not far off.'

Outside, a second van had pulled up alongside the Morris.

'The delivery men,' said Browne. 'And here

comes the plane.'

The twin-engined Douglas D-B-7 bomber sloped its way down to the far end of the runway and made a beautiful landing. It taxied around the crumbling perimeter track, then slowed to a halt about twenty yards away.

Browne had detached himself from Chris and White and was talking to the driver of the newly-arrived van. As he rejoined them, the van doors were opened and two blindfolded and handcuffed men were bundled out, onto the concrete of the dispersal point.

The door of the bomber was opened and steps were lowered.

The handcuffed men were hustled across the separating distance, and manhandled into the aircraft.

'Ah, well. Duty calls,' sighed Browne and led the way to the Douglas.

The two heavies Browne had called 'the delivery men' climbed from the bomber as Browne, White and Chris arrived.

One of them said, 'Goods slightly shop-soiled, sir.'

Browne nodded and said, 'Their own fault, no doubt. They *will* insist that they've cornered the market in roughing people up.'

The heavy growled some sort of agreement, then said, 'We'll be here when you get back, sir.'

Browne smiled, then led the way into the belly of the Douglas.

*   *   *

It was cold inside the Douglas. The door was open, and the slip-stream was like a solid wall of rushing air as it blasted down the outside of the fuselage. The engines and the air gave a background throb, but it was moderately easy to speak and be heard. A handful more decibels, but no more.

The two handcuffed men had had their blindfolds removed, but they remained sullenly silent on the seats to which they'd been locked; they'd been warned that too much talk or objections, and the blindfolds would be replaced, and, if necessary, with the addition of gags. They were anxious to know what was happening, and what was *going* to happen.

Browne had centre-stage, and he seemed to be rather enjoying himself.

He was saying, 'One union, you see. That's the final objective. One union, dealing with every aspect of energy. Coal, electricity, oil, gas, petrol, nuclear power. The whole shooting match. Then another super-union handling every aspect of communication. Radio, TV, newspapers, magazines, books, the cinema. There are far too many unions ... that's what our friends here believe. Massive closed shops. That's what *they* are after. After that ... forget democracy. Do as you're told—*exactly* as you're told ... or we'll close down the whole

254

nation. Believe what we tell you to believe ... because there's nothing else *to* believe.

'That's what these two beauties were working for. They're not the top men—the trade union barons, the genuine socialists ... but they control the barons and the politically motivated people.

'The king-makers. The powers behind various thrones. They, and their kind. The unknown masters who pull the strings. It pays. It's better—cheaper—than war. Get at the soft underbelly, and take a country over *that* way.'

He strolled to the open door of the plane and looked out. He seemed satisfied, returned to his previous place and continued, 'Kremlin sponsored, of course. The rent-a-crowd—the ragged-arsed revolutionaries—they have to be seen to. The placards have to be paid for. The liquid courage. The travelling expenses. Revolts cost money—especially if those who are revolting don't give a damn about what happens to anybody, other than themselves. The bully-boys. They're for hire. Always ... and only for hire. And scum like this...' He jerked a thumb in the direction of the handcuffed men. 'They hire. They organise. A few—a favoured few—take a periodic taxi-ride to Highgate and get their instructions, and their lolly, from the Russian residents there.'

He paused, and the elder of the two prisoners growled, 'I don't know who you are, but when we get back, I'll have your guts on a

255

plate. I'll...'

'*When* you get back,' sneered Browne. '*If* you get back.'

The elder prisoner closed his mouth, and the younger prisoner looked a little worried.

'Down there...' Browne motioned with his head. 'The Dogger Bank. Ten thousand feet below. Quite a drop.'

'You're bluffing,' snarled the elder prisoner.

'Your friend doesn't think so,' said Browne gently. 'Your friend is quite sure I'm *not* bluffing.'

The younger prisoner licked his lips, then stammered, 'Look—look ... why don't we...'

'Reach an agreement?' Browne raised his eyebrows.

'Yes.' The younger prisoner nodded eagerly. 'Yes. Something like that.'

'For you to back-pedal? Dismantle all the finely tuned outbreaks of violence?'

'Yeah. Yeah.' The younger man nodded again. Eagerly.

The elder prisoner said, 'We can't.'

'You mean, you *won't*?' said Browne.

'Same thing.'

'Not quite. The difference is between life and death.'

'We *can*,' babbled the young prisoner.

'*He* can,' teased Browne, to the elder prisoner.

'He daren't.'

'He daren't *not*. Ask him.'

'For Christ's sake!' The younger prisoner was almost sobbing.

The elder prisoner's lip curled and he said, 'I still think you're bluffing.'

'Instead of gulags,' murmured Browne. He jerked his head and spoke to Chris and White. 'This is about right. Get them to the door ... then we'll decide.'

There wasn't much of a struggle. The younger prisoner tried to back off, but handcuffed wrists limited his options. The elder prisoner didn't even do that. Maybe he thought the whole thing was still a bluff.

Less than two minutes later the two prisoners were standing, alongside each other near the door of the Douglas. The side draught from the slip-streams plucked at their clothes and Browne had to speak a little louder.

'Who do we dump?' he asked.

'Please. *Please!*' The younger prisoner looked ill.

'Can you unfix things?' asked Browne.

'Sure. Of course. Just let us...'

'Not "us". You?'

'Okay. I'll do it. Anything.'

The elder prisoner spat, 'You shithouse.'

'Isn't he?' Browne smiled then continued speaking to the younger prisoner. 'Bear things in mind. You have a wife and two sons. Next time you come, you'll be one of four. And you'll be the fourth to be thrown out.'

'Yeah. Yeah. Sure...' The man was openly

weeping. His knees were beginning to buckle.

'Dump him,' snapped Browne, and the order was quite sudden. Almost unexpected, after all the talk.

White and Chris grabbed the elder prisoner. One at each side. There was a moment's resistance, then it was too late. A short backward swing, then a forward heave, and the man started to scream.

The scream went on and on. Gradually dying away, but never dying away into silence. There was an echo, followed by an echo of the echo, followed by an echo of that echo. The everlasting tag end of the scream came up from the sea, bounced off the inside of the fuselage and raced round his skull. Never-ending. A scream of wheels within wheels; rippling, bouncing, recoiling and ricocheting ... but never granting the balm of complete silence.

1992

The Forton Service Area café was almost deserted. A heavy-lidded waitress stood behind the tea counter, waiting for customers. A youth whose hair was a little too long and a little too unruly swept between the tables and sought crumbs and tiny debris that wasn't really there. It was the 'dead-but-won't-lie-down' stretch of the day. Two HGV men scanned yesterday's newspapers and smoked cigarettes as a change from drinking lukewarm tea while they waited for their legally required period of 'rest' to come to an end.

Chris and Avril sat at a corner table, tasted moderately good coffee and exchanged what had once been closely guarded secrets.

Chris muttered, 'It's never gone away. Never silenced itself. A quarter of a century. More. And I still wake up in the night, hearing that bloody scream. Inside. Y'know—inside my head. I can hear it every time I think about throwing him out.'

'And yet,' mused Avril, 'you never asked about being taken off.'

'What?'

'The list of government killers.'

'What else? Marie's schooling had to be paid for.'

'Marie?' She sounded surprised.

'Schooling. University.' Then, in a slightly more eager tone, 'She earned a damn good B.Sc.'

'Good.'

'Then a Ph.D.'

'Fine.'

'She's—y'know—one of the top naturalists—botanists, what have you—in the country. Adviser to the Ministry, in fact.'

'You must be proud.'

'Yeah ... I suppose. Married. Two kids. But—y'know—it all cost money, so I had to

259

carry on doing it.'

'Killing people.'

'What the hell else?' The words became a little sour. 'My trade ... if I *have* a trade.'

'At any rate.' She sounded cheerful. 'The Calder Hall thing went off without a hitch. And nobody organised any super-unions.'

'I suppose,' he repeated glumly.

She teased the wrappings from a chocolate biscuit and asked, 'How many killings, so far?'

'I didn't keep a tally. I did what I was told.'

'But for almost a quarter of a century. They must have mounted up.'

'I suppose,' he said for a third time. 'I reckon twenty ... thereabouts. Browne could have told you.'

'He's dead now, of course.'

'Almost two years ago.' His lips gave a quick sardonic twitch. 'As I understand it, the bastard died in bed.'

'Natural causes.' She bit into the biscuit. 'A sudden, unexpected heart attack.'

'Lucky.'

'Whereas you ...' She chewed biscuit as she spoke. 'You're still haunted by that first government killing you carried out.'

'The others were all long-distance,' he grunted. 'Rifle. Handgun. That was the only hands-on job I did.'

'Tell me about some of the others,' she invited, then stood up from the table and added, 'But wait until I've been for

260

a couple of refills.'

                    *   *   *

They sipped coffee and nibbled biscuits until
dawn and, slowly at first, but with what seemed
to be an increasing eagerness, he unburdened
himself. No pattern. Nothing ordered or
chronological. Just a jumble of names; men
who had been on the periphery of spy scandals;
political jackals who had planned for power
and corruption; bombers and political
butchers wily enough to stay outside the reach
of the orthodox law. A quick shot from an
overtaking car. A bullet in the back in some
unlighted alley. 'Distance' killings. Nothing
'hands-on' ... except that first dumping over
the North Sea.

'The worst of the lot,' he confessed. 'I don't
think I could have stuck it if they'd all been like
that.'

'And yet, it didn't upset either White or
Browne,' she mused.

'Maybe not. I wouldn't know.'

He rhapsodised about other aspects of his
life; the Yorkshire moorlands and dales; the
basic beauty of living alone in the caravan; the
silent magnificence of personal solitude.

'You can think. No distractions. Read a
little, walk a little, get to know certain
fumdamental truths. Sir Andrew was fixed—I
don't know how—and he never asked

261

questions. I did a gamekeeping job for him. He deserved that. But he couldn't sack me. He made that clear in a dozen different ways. But—y'know—I tried to play fair with him.'

'I'm sure you did.'

'I wasn't employed at any of the shoots. Not even as a beater. I was like a bloody hermit ... but that's the way I wanted it.'

The cold dawn crept up over Bowland Forest, but still he talked. Like a leaking faucet; not gushing, not even continuous ... but quietly—softly—as if he was talking to himself. As if he was gradually and gently relieving himself of any impossible, pent-up pressure.

'I was never ill. An odd cold—a bit of a sniffle—but never more than that. No medicine. A few extra lungfuls of good, Yorkshire air. A brisk walk. Then I'd be as right as rain. Never ill. I sometimes wondered what it would be like to be ill. To need a doctor, maybe. Even hospital. Not that I wanted to be ill. Just that I was sometimes curious.'

'No friends?' she murmured.

'Friends?' His mouth twisted. 'I kill friends ... remember? Jared. Morven never came again. I sometimes wished ... But she didn't. Queenie and Daisy died while I was at war. I never bothered with any other animal.' A pause, then, 'who the hell needs friends? As I see things, they let you down. No friends ... nobody lets you down.' A pause, a mouthful of

262

coffee and a bite into a biscuit, then, 'The parson tried to be my friend. The local Holy Joe. Tried to sell me God. The truth is, I knew more about God than he did. God was out there, on the moors ... not in some dusty village church. And, whenever I killed, I *was* God. Pity I couldn't tell him that. But—I suppose—he wouldn't have understood. To him—y'know—it was just a job. But to me, it was obvious. I *knew*.'

They left the service area and drove north, to junction thirty-three, then south again and towards Blackpool. Back the way they'd come, then the branch right along the spur motorway. And still, he talked. Repeating himself sometimes, because he was an old man, and not used to long conversations. Not even one-sided conversations.

And gradually, the talk became punctuated by longer and longer silences. The words became a little like scatterings of rice, to be carefully gathered into tiny heaps before use.

'Seth was an evil bastard. I didn't realise it then ... but I realise it now. He liked killing things. Enjoyed himself, whenever he could destroy something.'

'Perhaps.' She didn't sound too sure.

'He gave Aunt Mabel hell.'

'That, I believe.'

'He deserved his own end.'

'If you say so.'

They drove through Blackpool from the

263

rear; from the rows of once-upon-a-time boarding houses that now luxuriated in the grander name of 'private hotels'; towards the back of the Tower, then out onto the front. A cold, early-morning front. A near-deserted promenade, scoured by wind-blown sand. She turned left and drove towards St Annes.

'I think I rather liked Browne.'

'He'd have appreciated that.'

'A professional. I like professionalism. It's a rare quality.'

'Rare,' she agreed.

'And White, come to that. He could be relied upon. Nice guy. I'd have liked to have known him a little better.'

'They—those two—they were your friends,' she suggested. 'The only friends you allowed yourself.'

'And Marie, of course. Always Marie.'

'Marie was your surrogate daughter.' She spoke with absolute certainty. 'She calls you "uncle", but you're more than that.'

'I reckon,' he agreed.

The silence lasted longer this time. It lasted while she drove south, past the piers, past the holiday camp and along the promenade until she'd braked on the car park alongside the beach.

She said, 'A walk on the sands to blow the cobwebs away.'

He climbed out. She, too, climbed out and, before she locked the door, she slipped the .25

hammerless Colt automatic pistol from the glove compartment and slipped it into the pocket of her fur coat.

They walked slowly; across the firm, wet sand and into the cold morning breeze. His replies, when he made them, were little more than grunts. They were alone. Just the two of them, in a flat, featureless world populated only by themselves and the sea birds.

She said, 'His name—if you're interested—was Evans. Welsh, of course, but you knew that. The man you knew as "White". Evans. He's dead, too. A road accident.'

'You know these things?'

'Those war years. Remember? 1940? When I first picked you up? Remember Ridgeway?'

'The Flight Lieutenant?'

'He was right in his spot assessment. A natural.'

'A natural what?'

'Killer. Not yet twenty, but you were anxious to kill Germans. You didn't know the ins and outs of the war ... but you wanted to kill people.'

'Is that right?' He sounded quite indifferent.

'Dansey spotted it. That's why you were chosen.'

'And you?'

'To keep an eye on you, for the benefit of Commander Morton, RN.'

'Who the hell's...'

'You knew him as "Browne".'

'You mean...'

'Father. My father. Like Dansey ... a government "fixer".'

He didn't answer. Instead he walked, head bent, into the breeze. Slowly. Like a self-activating robot.

She continued, 'Pollard hated you. With reason. You were Dansey's star turn. You could have ousted Pollard, had you wanted to.' A dozen or so silent steps forward, then, 'All these years, Chris. You've been led by the nose.'

He began to scowl, as if forcing certain unpleasant—unacceptable—thoughts to enter his mind.

Still in a slow, conversational tone, she said, 'Once upon a time I almost loved you. Then I almost hated you ... when you dropped me like a brick, after the war. Then when I took over father's job...'

'*You* took over...'

'Why not? You've been out of it for a long, long time, but take it from me. Women have complete equality these days. Even in the so-called "Secret Service". He confided in me ... therefore when he died, I was the natural choice.'

'*You're* "Browne"?' He still seemed to have difficulty in accepting what she was saying.

'*Mrs* Browne,' she said with a tight smile. Then, 'And I don't have to tell you what you've done ... do I?'

'Spilled my guts.' He stopped, bent his head slightly more and stared at the toes of his boots. 'The lot. Like a spoiled teenager. Like a...'

'Like a weary man who yearns for rest,' she said gently.

'Maybe,' he muttered.

'Know the truth, Chris.' There was affection in her tone. 'Pollard was never a threat to *me*. He never cared about Marie. *I* saved *you* from him. But,' she added, 'It was nice thinking you were trying to shield me.'

'A complete muggins,' he breathed.

'Things are never as they should be. Never as they seem ... especially in this game.'

The name 'Marie' came out on a breath, as he dropped on one knee.

She had the Colt in her hand and she placed the snout against the nape of his neck.

'It won't hurt,' she promised softly. 'It won't last long enough to hurt.'

As she squeezed the trigger, he heard the last echoes of the scream inside his head. Saw the face of Hess, smiling or smirking. He hadn't time to decide which.

*   *   *

In the close-knit community of Lytham St Annes, it was a short-lived talking point. A body, on the beach. Some unknown man shot through the neck.

267

Why? ... A dozen guesses, none correct and nothing within a mile of the truth.

There was an inquest. For some months the body was kept in cold storage, pending police enquiries. The enquiries led nowhere.

High summer arrived, the coroner released the body, and there was a funeral; a hole, dug in the ground of the parish graveyard, and a ceremony attended by a handful of people. People from the hall, a middle-aged woman who'd travelled from down south, and an elderly woman who was a stranger.

The two women moved towards each other as they left the grave.

'Marie?' asked the elder woman.

'Yes.' The younger woman looked a little puzzled.

'Avril.' The older woman introduced herself. 'I knew him in the war years.'

'Oh.'

'Not well, of course. But enough to know he was unique.'

'Unique?' The puzzled look deepened.

'Unusual.'

'I'd have called him "good". He was unusually good, if that's what you mean.'

'Perhaps.' Avril smiled. 'Perhaps that's what I *do* mean. An unusually *good* man.'

We hope you have enjoyed this Large Print book. Other Chivers Press or G. K. Hall Large Print books are available at your library or directly from the publishers. For more information about current and forthcoming titles, please call or write, without obligation, to:

Chivers Press Limited
Windsor Bridge Road
Bath BA2 3AX
England
Tel. (01225) 335336

OR

G. K. Hall
P.O. Box 159
Thorndike, Maine 04986
USA
Tel. (800) 223–6121 (U.S. & Canada)
In Maine call collect: (207) 948–2962

All our Large Print titles are designed for easy reading, and all our books are made to last.